FIEND
IN THE
FOREST

LEE DAWSON

FIEND IN THE FOREST

THE **LOST GORGE** MYSTERIES

A Small-Town Mystery

Published by Elite Edition 2022
First edition by Elite Edition 2019 as Winter Stalker

Cover image ©2022 Shutterstock Riku Mannisto

Paperback ISBN: 9798358763326

Second edition

This book was professionally typeset on Reedsy.

Find out more at reedsy.com

Chapter 1

The blizzard had descended on the Lost Gorge Mountain Resort with winds so fierce employee Mina Park couldn't gauge from which direction the storm emanated. Snowfall amounts were impossible to determine. What lay on the ground swirled in a dance with what still fell from the sky.

Mina operated a chairlift on top of a peak, fittingly called Baldie. On a good day, she could see for miles. Today she had trouble finding her feet. The storm had started with a drenching rain that had frozen the snow under the lift.

As she repeatedly struck the ice under the chairlift with a shovel to give riders some traction, she contemplated all the bad life decisions that had led her to this miserable day. A smarter woman would regret them; Mina clung to them.

By three, the blizzard's contrary nature had left the mountain almost empty. Even the most hardened skiers and boarders abandoned the slopes, frustrated at conditions that meant fresh powder for a few feet and exposed ice for a lot more.

The resort had sent word they were shutting down the lift a few minutes early due to wind. "This isn't wind," Mina muttered as the radio crackled the news. "This is a freaking end-of-days cyclone."

A chair carrying two snowboarders broke through the storm. As she exited the unheated lift house, a small building no bigger than a shed with windows lining one side, Mina plastered on a warm smile that did not reach her numbed toes. The boarders scooted off as she wished them a good day.

Go home, she thought. *It's not worth riding in this weather.*

All she wanted was to finish the day and go home to a hot bath. She'd left Dakdoritang, a spicy Korean stew and an old family recipe, in the slow cooker and longed to be warm and full.

Her radio buzzed with static. "Mina?" Tim, a liftie at the bottom of the mountain, broke through the static. "Ski patrol says to close down. I just loaded the last rider."

"Hallelujah," she said out loud but without pushing the radio button. Mina didn't usually work the lifts, but an early-season flu had wiped out some of the staff. With very few guests being in need of a ski instructor that morning, she'd been called up.

"He's on chair 61. Over."

"Ten-four." With her day finally ending, she could almost smell dinner.

She blinked the snowflakes out of her eyes as each chair crept out of the cold inferno before turning to make its long journey down. It fell to her and Tim to make sure the lift was empty of guests before she could catch her own chair down. If she hurried with the last rider and locking up, she could make it on chair 70.

Chair 59 appeared, and she counted down her day, 3...2...then chair 61 appeared through the low clouds, empty.

Chair 62 followed, also empty. She counted five chairs before she grabbed the radio. "Tim, you read wrong; chair 61 was empty."

Static filled the silent air. Mina kept her eyes on the chairs; maybe he meant 71. All passed empty, and the numbers started at one again. She tried again with the radio.

This time Tim responded. "Confirm, last rider on chair 61."

"Confirmed, no one was on it." She didn't bother to conceal the annoyance in her voice. Her foot warmers had long worn out.

"I didn't imagine someone getting on," Tim argued.

"And I haven't taken my eyes off the chairlift since you radioed. No one has come up."

Chair 61 went by again, still empty.

Dread replaced the feeling of cold. "Call ski patrol. We've got a possible fall."

Mina watched the chairs a minute longer, silently begging the rider to come out of the darkness. When they didn't, she grabbed her skis, not waiting for ski patrol. If someone had fallen off, she was the closest person to find them. She volunteered for the county Search and Rescue team, and no way she'd let somebody lie hurt in a blizzard.

The storm had only grown worse in the ticking minutes she'd waited for the rider to appear. She rushed to shut everything down and strap on her ski boots. The stiff, cold plastic protested as she pried the opening in the boot as far as she could and wedged her foot in. Each boot took a few minutes—much too long.

There were parts of the lift where if a person fell off, they'd land in a pile of snow and receive a bruised rear. But there were long stretches between cliffs and over ravines where a slip could mean death. If someone out there lay injured, she'd be racing against the storm to find them.

She strapped on a vest with a few essentials and a radio stuck to the front, then stomped her feet in each ski and pushed off with her poles. This lift accessed two separate groomed runs and a lot more tree trails. She made a beeline for the trail under the lift. There would be no following it straight down as the lift went over a few cliffs.

The trail, rated a black diamond in good conditions, which that day was decidedly not, led her to the edge of the first cliff. Ski patrol had placed a fence warning skiers and riders to make a hard turn to avoid a quick death. The face was nothing but granite rock, invisible from where she stood. There were a couple of spots where the chairlift came within fifteen feet of the ground. In some places, a rider could reach out and touch a tree.

Above her, a few chairs swung in the wind, bouncing and squeaking. Her eyes followed the line of the chairlift through the whiteness, straining to see anyone on the ground. Between gusts of wind, the next ridgeline appeared. In between the two ridges was a bowl tailor-made for powder skiing.

As she was about to push off to go around the cliff, a flash of movement caught her eye. Something moved from tree to tree on the distant ridge not far from the chairlift. It moved with a deliberate pace, not the skittishness of an animal.

She shoved off, skidding down the side until she could drop into the bowl below the rock face. Mina reached the other side of the bowl where she could exit to the right and jump out on a run below. But the movement had been above her in the trees. She clicked off her skis and stuck them straight up in the snow.

The winds changed direction, picking up speed from the north. She had minutes before the heaviest snow would fall. The first part of the storm had only been a prelude to the main event.

Several high pine trees lined the edge of the bowl and the cliffs above. "Hello," she yelled into the wind. The storm pushed the words back down her throat, and she gasped for air. "Anyone there?" She tried again and louder.

The storm made it seem as if Mina was the only human left on the mountain. If someone had fallen here, she didn't see any signs, though this wind would make quick work of any tracks.

A large shadow moved in the trees up a fifteen-foot embankment. She went to call out a third time but hesitated. Wind blew the tree branches, making everything come alive. The shadow, however, moved through the trees at a steady pace until it faded.

If someone had fallen, why would they climb up there? Common sense would lead them downhill, toward the ski run.

Mina wanted to call out, should've called out. Instead, she stepped backward, incredibly aware of how alone she was, until she bumped into her skis. Fear, rarely felt even standing on the edge of a cliff ready to ski off, flowed through her.

She couldn't identify what caused such a visceral reaction, and weakness angered her more than the fear overwhelmed her. "Stop it," she said aloud. "Don't be an idiot."

Grasping a thin aspen tree jutting out of the ground, she pulled herself partway up the embankment. Her arms shook at carrying her weight, and she tried to grip the snow with her boots. With no flex in her ski boots, she slid down. On her second attempt, she lunged and grasped a higher tree.

She succeeded, reaching the first of the pines.

She yanked her snow-covered goggles up onto her helmet and squinted, trying to spot movement amongst the trees' shadows.

"Hello," she yelled out. "Is anyone here?" Only rushing the wind through the treetops broke the quiet stillness.

She took a few halting steps but sank into the soft snow. She fumbled, trying to stop her descent, but with nothing solid to grasp on to, she fell face-first into the snow. Like a drowning person trying to tread water, she struggled to get vertical.

A loud thud echoed through the forest, vibrating the trees so much the snow perched on the branches dropped to the ground.

Mina froze as her glance shot around the forest. A few summers ago, she'd hiked along a river and experienced the prickly sensation of being watched. After a half-mile, she'd glimpsed a black bear on a ridge stalking.

That feeling returned in force, multiplied by the precarious position she held. At least then she had bear spray; now she wore boots impossible to run in.

"Bears are in hibernation," she whispered in a futile attempt to reassure herself. "Nobody has ever seen one at the resort during winter." But she couldn't shake the instinct something tracked her.

Mina found her footing and took a few steps backward, using the heel of her boot to break through the snow. The ground shook with a loud bang like a giant pine snapping in the storm. The wind grew stronger, ushering a high-pitched screaming sound that was neither human nor animal

She backed up several steps, not daring to call out again. She fell backward over the small ledge she'd just climbed up, tumbling over the snow and bushes. Above her, the wind, or something else, blew its fury through the trees.

She'd shaken off steeper falls than that and jumped to her feet. The pine branches spread parted in opposite directions; something was coming through.

Mina slammed her boots against her ski bindings, freeing chunks of snow, and snapped in. With one more glimpse at the parting trees, she pushed off.

5

Her skis never turned until she hit the open run below.

Fog had set in and, despite being on a run she'd taken hundreds of times, she could only determine uphill from downhill by her speed. Sleet filled her eyes, and she yanked her goggles back down but they were caked in snow. She ripped them off.

Mina skidded to a stop, seconds away from crashing into the lodge. Its stone walls blended into the gray sky, rendering it nearly invisible.

A red-jacketed ski patroller came out of the grayness from the direction of the chairlift. "Mina." Patrick Orrick, a friend and more than occasional date, called out to her. With his goggles and helmet, she only recognized him from the bushy auburn beard now filled with ice. "Tim told me about the missing guest. I came down the run with a snowmobile but didn't see anything. You?"

In the presence of another human, Mina's paranoia receded into shame. She considered the howling in the woods and the loud bangs. "I thought I did, but it was only the wind in the trees. Is Tim sure someone got on the chairlift?"

"He isn't 100 percent sure which chair, but swears a guy got on right before he radioed you." Patrick pulled his goggles up. "How sure are you no one got off?"

"100 percent," she said without hesitation. They both scanned the dark clouds circling the mountain. As a search and rescue volunteer, Mina knew risks had to be taken to save lives, but they should be calculated risks.

She calculated the risk and didn't like the summation. "What are we going to do?"

Patrick squeezed out the snow accumulating in his beard. "The weather is calling for two feet by morning. If someone is up there, they won't survive this."

"Then we find them tonight." Shame at abandoning the mountain seeped through her like the cold.

Patrick gestured to the lodge. "Sheriff just got here. Let's see what he says."

Mina didn't want to ask; she wanted to go back up but couldn't alone. Snow pummeled the mountain as the last of their light slipped away. Waiting would turn a rescue into a recovery by morning.

Chapter 2

Lodge was a loose term to describe the stone building that sat at the base of the resort. It held no lodging, only a locker room and a small restaurant that specialized in burgers and not much else.

Mina walked into the restaurant with Patrick. The door slammed behind them like the storm wanted the mountain to itself. Sheriff Solo Chapa, or Sol as everyone called him, stood in front of a detailed topographical map laid out on a table. All the guests had long since called it a day.

Without looking up, Sol said. "Mina, show me where you think the skier could be."

Up until a year or so ago, Sol had commanded the Search and Rescue or SAR unit. SAR was a volunteer group under the sheriff. Mina had volunteered the last five years when she was in town. When the sheriff's position unexpectedly opened, the town council had urged Sol to take over until a proper election could be held.

Mina joined him at the map. It took all of her patience to not yell at him and Patrick they were losing daylight and their chance. Had it been anyone else but Sol, she would not have held her tongue. That man could find a particular snowflake in a blizzard. He knew the country and had the ability to predict human behavior in it.

It took a few minutes to orientate herself to the map; it only showed the lines of elevation and not the lifts. Baldie was where she'd been posted; she found that first. Taking a marker, she drew a line from the peak to the bottom where the lift ran.

After that, she could follow her path down the mountain until her finger stopped at the trees at the bottom of the bowl. "I maybe saw something there. We need to get up there now."

"What did you see?"

Had she really seen anything? There had been no tracks in that grove.

"Something moving. I don't know what."

"You don't think it was the lost skier?"

"Not sure, but you can't get there by falling or skiing. He'd have to have climbed up."

"So where is the skier?"

"I tried to follow the chairlift as much as I could and didn't see anyone. But visibility was sometimes only twenty feet or so."

Patrick looked over their shoulders. "Me and a couple of my guys took snowmobiles up and down the runs but didn't spot anything. But like Mina said, visibility sucked. We crawled our way down and were lucky not to go over a cliff."

Sol stared out the huge picture windows lining the restaurant. Usually, a person could enjoy lunch with a view of the mountains, at least on a clear day. That day it viewed a vast gray rapidly turning black.

"If he fell and knocked himself out, he'd be covered by snow in a few minutes." Patrick continued. "There'd be nothing to see. I've got a few ski patrollers out around the base, but I'm not sending any more people up, not in this."

Sol shook his head. "No, we don't want to lose anyone else."

Mina glanced between the two men. "You can't mean we leave him out there." Her voice rose in volume. "He'll be dead by morning."

"Mina," Sol said.

"No, I can ski that line again. There are a couple of ravines he could've fallen in."

Sol pointed to the large windows. "Look out there. Can you even see the chairlift? I've been in storms like this. You can't find the ground underneath you, can't tell whether you're facing uphill or down. I don't want you or anyone else lost until spring."

Mina's jaw clenched. "So, we leave them out there to die?"

"No…" At Mina's hard stare, Sol stopped. "Yes, we risk that. But I won't kill you to save someone else." Sol took a step closer and lowered his voice. "I've known you long enough to know that at heart you are a rescuer. And I know this goes against every instinct you have. But you have to learn when to commit and when to wait."

"Plus, we can't say for sure someone is even out there," Patrick said. "How many riders jump off the lift when it gets close to the cliffs and ski down?"

She considered that. YouTube was filled with videos of people making the jump. She herself had done it but wasn't stupid enough to post it and cost her a job. "But not usually this early. The base is shallow, making the jump farther and harder."

"I pull people off the mountain every day doing stupid stuff, Mina. If they did, they could be hurt or they could've landed it."

"All the more reason not to risk any more lives," Sol said. "We wait until morning."

Mina knew they spoke the truth, but she also knew in a way she couldn't explain that someone was out there. She'd had one chance to ski that mountain and find the missing skier but let her own fears stop her; she had failed.

If someone died, it would be on her.

Chapter 3

Mina stood in the storm, the cold coursing through her body and freezing the blood within her veins. The lifts were stopped, and the world shrank to the ten or so feet she could see.

Sol stepped out of the lodge. "I could use your help during the winter. Clint wants to take some time off when the baby comes. You're still sworn in. I know you said—"

"I said no."

During the last summer, the rivers had run low and rafting slowed down, costing her a job as a guide. To make ends meet, or at least come closer together, Mina had taken a temporary job as a deputy for the sheriff. She'd helped out at the harvest festival, directing traffic and picking up trash. Her one exciting moment had been breaking up a fight between two drunks, who were twice her size.

"It wouldn't be full-time," Sol said. "Just think about it."

"Okay." She wouldn't.

"I'm going to plan out tomorrow's search with Patrick. Can you go through the parking lot and see what cars are left? Maybe if we have an abandoned car, we'll have an idea if someone is up there."

"Yeah, the employees still working will all be parked in one spot. I can see who else is left."

In the parking lot, Mina used her phone to snap pics of each car, along with a close-up of the license plate. She'd made it about two-thirds of the way through the parking lot when she found a couple of snowboarders sitting on the tailgate of a truck, putting on their shoes.

"Hey," she called out as she walked toward them. They looked at her suspiciously. She realized she spoke with an authoritative tone but didn't wear a uniform or anything to back the tone up. "I work here."

One slipped a silver can behind him. "We were heading home." He wore a patched-up coat and pants with duct tape across his knees.

The other one held up a cell phone. "We lost track of our buddy. Been trying to call him."

"When?"

He stuttered a bit at her abrupt tone. "Afternoon, three or four."

"Can you come with me back to the lodge? The sher—" She thought better. "The Search and Rescue commander is there, and I'd like him to know there's a boarder missing." Seeing how nervous they'd been at her seeing the beer can, she didn't want to scare them off.

"I don't know if it's that big of deal," said the one in patched-up pants. "He'll turn up, tends to take off occasionally." They jumped off the tailgate and turned toward the cab.

"We're actually looking for a missing boarder. Someone loaded the chairlift but never made it to the top," Mina said.

The men turned in unison. One stood open-mouthed while Patches let loose a torrent of curses at the missing friend. He pulled out his cell and made a call, but evidently got voicemail. "Jason, call me back, man. Now. No more of this."

Neither of the men argued with Mina as she led them back to the lodge.

Sol still sat in the empty restaurant, pencil in hand, making notes on the map. He glanced up when the three of them walked into the room.

"These guys lost their friend around three or four," Mina said. "His name is Jason ..." she turned to the two guys, "what's the last name?"

"Collins," Patches said. "Jason Collins."

Sol stood. "I'm Sheriff Chapa. Where did you last see him?"

"We got on the Lucky Jack lift and then got separated on the way down." Lucky Jack ran on the other side of the resort from Summit.

"He talk about making a run on this side of the mountain?" Mina asked.

They turned to her, looked down at her, then back to Sol. "We were planning on skiing the entire mountain. Didn't want to repeat a run."

Sol took a step back and glanced over at Mina, silently asking her to take over. He knew she spoke these boys' language better than he.

"I'm Mina Park, deputy." She stared straight into their eyes without flinching, hoping they wouldn't notice her uncertainty. "Did you plan on meeting Jason at the bottom of the lift after the run? Is it common for him to go off without you?"

"We just said something about racing to the bottom. We got down, and he wasn't there so we figured he went back up."

"What run did you take down?"

"Didn't take a run. We dropped down Corner Chute." Chutes were steep gullies and usually lined with rock, at least in Lost Gorge.

If she wanted these guys to pay attention, she had to admire their riding and show she knew what she was talking about. "Did you run into that patch of ice after the first pitch? I wiped out on that a few days ago. Rolled down about fifty feet."

Patches stood straighter. "About did but skirted the edge and dropped farther down the ridge." Sol sat on a nearby table, scribbling notes.

"What was Jason wearing?"

The one looked down at his own clothes as if that could give him a clue. The other one shrugged. "Don't know. Maybe a blue or a black coat."

"Was he boarding or skiing?"

"Boarding, like us. Just got a new Burton board; it's got this crazy graphic of a beast looking over the mountains."

Had Tim mentioned the missing person was a boarder or a skier? She'd assumed skier but didn't know for sure.

"Yeah." The buddy jumped in. "It's mostly black and gray, but underneath is red. Jason saved his tip money from guiding in the summer to buy it." His voice went quiet. "Today was his first day on it."

People might judge someone for dropping $500 on a new piece of gear while wearing pants duct-taped together. Those people were not Mina. "You try texting him?"

"Tried to, but the texts bounced back." Cell phone service was known to be unreliable at best in this corner of the mountains. "I figured if we lost him, he'd turn up at the truck but nobody was there."

They said Jason was originally from Wisconsin, He'd come West after college to drop down the steeps of the Rockies before he would settle into a real job after a gap year. Mina had done the same thing ten years ago, but the real job had never panned out. She worked winter seasons at the resort, summers wherever jobs were, and wandered the in-between times.

Mina took their numbers and promised to call if they found anything. They promised to call if they heard from him.

By the time they left, it was long dark outside. "Go home," Sol told Mina. "Get some sleep. When the storm breaks, we'll be out there. Even if it's dark, least we can do is take one of the Cats down the run. Might see something."

The Cat referred to the large groomers that went down the ski runs each night to smooth out the snow. "I skied down the runs where they cross under the lift, Sol. If he fell in a place a Cat can get to, I would've seen him. If someone is there, he would be in the backcountry in the trees."

"We'll do everything we can."

She hated that statement. Sometimes everything they could do wasn't enough. Three seasons ago, the SAR team spent a week searching for a four-year-old who'd wandered away from the camp. They'd never found him, and she still dreamed that little boy called out to her.

Mina trudged through the snow to the parking lot where the storm had already left several inches on her car. That morning in anticipation, she'd pulled her wipers away from her windshield to keep them from being iced over, but it still required a good amount of effort to scrape the ice off. She'd forgotten her mittens, and it took more than a few minutes to get feeling back in her fingers even in her warming Jeep.

A few minutes in the snow and her hands were already numb. How long could someone lost in the storm survive?

Chapter 4

The second Mina walked through the door of her home, she turned on the electric space heater to vanquish the cold air.

Her place, a studio apartment, wasn't much but at least she didn't share it with five other instructors like a lot of her coworkers. Real estate came cheap in the town of Lost Gorge, but so did seasonal salaries.

Mina's room resided in what had been a large mansion built at the turn of the century by a mine owner who'd struck it rich in silver. Within a year of moving in, the mines dried up, striking him as poor just as quickly. The opulent house had served a series of purposes over the last 100 years until her landlord had purchased it and converted each floor into two studio apartments, making six units.

The second she walked in the door, the red chili spices of the Dakdoritang overwhelmed her, and for a brief moment, she relaxed in the warmth of being home. That second passed too quickly as the events of the day set on her. She knew there would be no sleep tonight.

She dished out the stew made from a recipe passed on by her grandmother and was supposed to be passed on to Mina's own kids one day. As if on cue, her phone rang—her mother. She didn't have the heart for a conversation tonight. Her mother would ask about her day, and Mina would lie. Otherwise, it would turn into an argument about the direction her life was going, which wasn't anywhere. Even Mina could admit that; she just didn't care.

She'd come to Lost Gorge, a graduate fresh out of college but deep in the recession. Majoring in political science was supposed to launch her into law school but watching all her lawyer friends graduate neck-high in debt and jobless, Mina decided she was done with school. It seemed like doubling down on a bad bet. The only problem was that the undergrad degree didn't really mean much on its own.

Mina had looked into instructing at Bear Mountain and some of the other SoCal resorts but lack of snow that season meant lack of opportunity. A posting for instructors in the faraway town of Lost Gorge in the northern Rockies had beckoned, and she took it.

It was supposed to be a seasonal job and a gap year until she figured out her career. That gap had turned into ten.

It didn't matter. She valued a nomad's life. One summer she even chased winter all year bouncing from the States to New Zealand. She wouldn't even sign a six-month lease to save $50 a month, way too much commitment. The only long-term commitment she'd made in her life was to that worthless four-year degree she still paid loans on and the four months she taught skiing each winter, which paid better than the rest of the year.

The phone rang again. Sol's number popped up, and she answered. "What's up?"

"Just checked the latest weather. The storm's stalled out. There won't be any searching before morning. We'll be lucky if we're searching before noon." The frustration in his voice echoed through the phone. "But I want the crew up there by dawn so that we're mobile the second there's any break in the snow."

"I'll be there."

"You give any more thought to my offer?"

"Sol," she said with no small amount of exasperation.

"I'm sorry," Sol said. "Just because I didn't have much of a choice in being sheriff doesn't mean I get to take away yours."

She forgave him. He was one of those people who gave everything and got nothing. A quality she didn't want to entirely emulate. "I can keep working on-call, but I don't know about permanent."

"Do you still have the paperwork I gave you?"

She glanced at the drawer where she'd stuffed the forms in an attempt to ignore them. "Yeah."

"Then it's up to you, and I won't bring it up again until you decide. Have a good night."

State law required all its deputies to go through eight weeks of police training within a year of taking the job. She'd received some initial firearm training and such but needed to be certified. When she'd accepted the temp position, Mina had no intention of sticking with it. Told herself she was just helping Sol out for a few months.

It did offer health insurance and, after her ski injury a few seasons ago, she was more breakable. But if she did the training, she had to commit to the job for at least a year or pay back the cost of instruction. A year was a long time.

The job was another reason she didn't take her mother's call. Nobody outside the town knew she moonlighted as a cop. The way her parents worried, Mina didn't know if being a stripper or a police officer would be more welcome news.

She kept the drawer and its decision shut. There'd be time enough to think about it after they found the missing snowboarder.

* * *

Mina was up far before the sun, which didn't matter much. Even when dawn came, the storm would hold them hostage. What little sleep she'd managed was filled with shadows in the snow. Sometimes she called out to someone unseen, trying to help. Other times, she ran away, the deep snow hindering her escape.

By 5 am and thanks to four-wheel drive, she sat in the parking lot of the resort, hoping for a break in the storm, but instead watched other cars trickle in. The parking lot had been empty when she pulled in. If someone had spent the night out there, they hadn't left a car behind.

The resort had delayed opening any lifts due to the wind, but the parking lot was still half full by nine. Once the lifts opened, half the town would vie over first chair and the chance to make fresh tracks in the powder.

About ten or so people from SAR and ski patrol hovered in one corner of the lodge. Several ski patrollers, including Patrick, had already gone out. With dynamite tucked in their vests, they would ride snowmobiles to the peaks and bowls.

Every fifteen minutes or so the windows would shake at a boom that echoed across the lower valley. The hope was that these explosions would bring down the avalanches before people could. They would not be setting them off on Baldie lift for fear of covering up the missing person.

The skiers could wait all they wanted to, but the resort wouldn't open much terrain today.

At about ten the winds died down, and the resort agreed to open one lift to get the search going. With totals of 22 inches at the base and several feet at the top, no one held much hope of stumbling across anyone before June.

Mina clicked into her fattest skis, chosen for their ability to float on the powder. The ride up the chairlift with Sol made for a slow trip as they scanned the ground for any sign of life, or anything really.

"There," she said about halfway up, pointing at the cliff that came only fifteen or so feet below them. "I saw the movement in the trees on the other side."

As they crested the ridge, they came in view of the bowl Mina had planned to revisit. Sol jabbed his pole in the direction of the highest point of the bowl. "We come down there, we bring an avalanche down." The wind had blown the snow into an overhang over the edge. You wouldn't know it, skiing on top, which was where Mina usually dropped in.

"We can drop in closer to the lift. The pitch isn't as steep," Mina said.

They unloaded, and Mina waved at Tim who operated the lift. She dropped into the trees on the same trail as last night with Sol following. Sol skied, everyone in Lost Gorge did, but not at the same level as Mina. When they reached the edge of the bowl, her previous tracks were long since covered.

With the ledge too precarious to ski off, they stayed lower. The storm had come in with wet and heavy snow, which had frozen before the powder fell on top. This created two separate layers and a higher likelihood of sliding.

"I'll go first," she said. She knew the resort and its temperamental ways.

"Stay in my tracks when you follow."

Mina didn't make it more than 30 feet before the snow cracked, separating a distinct top layer from the bottom. She stopped, her knees leaning into the hill to give her skis more edge to grip the mountain.

"Don't come down," she said loud enough for Sol to hear but hopefully not loud enough to create a vibration. Below her lay the bowl; no trees could protect her from what was about to happen.

Had her feet not been clamped into ski boots, they'd be shaking.

Skiing forward would require her to cross snow on the cusp of a slide. It didn't need to be avalanche size; a foot could push her off the ledge. Going back would be more difficult and time-consuming, but it would lead her to the rock and relative safety from avalanches.

All of this debating took less than two seconds. Mina shoved off, pointing her skis in a straight line across and out of the slide's path. The deep snow flew out behind her in a wake. The slide tugged on her tips, threatening to pull her down, but she didn't dare turn.

The other side of the slope turned slightly uphill and into the trees. She didn't stop until she was surrounded by trees and on the next ridge. Only then did she look behind her. A chunk of snow about twenty feet wide and a foot deep had broken away from its foundation. The last little bit rolled into a ravine.

Sol waved from the other side and she waved back, signaling she was okay. But Mina was far from okay.

The trees she stopped in blocked out the little light of day. The only noise was the snap of branches as they broke under the heavy snow. Taking off her skis would sink her into the powder and probably over her head. She pulled off her goggles to get a better look at her surroundings. Trees and snow and not much else.

Mina stood about fifty above where she'd searched yesterday. Her radio buzzed.

"You okay?" Sol asked.

"Just lost a year of my life but other than that, sure."

"I'll follow."

"No, not until they do avalanche control."

"You sure?"

"I'm only 50 yards from the run. The slope isn't steep enough to slide after this."

"Still, get out of there."

"On my way, after I look around for a second." She wouldn't let fear push her out again.

After tucking the radio into her vest, she dropped into yesterday's grove. Once she reached it, the hill flattened and she sunk into the snow, her skis buried. She shuffled through the trees, breaking fresh snow with each hard-earned step.

She inhaled and with the scent of wet pine came something bitter and strong enough she could taste decay. As she moved across the terrain, the smell grew more pungent. Trying not to breathe failed as the difficult slog burned her lungs.

At its base, each pine had a hole under the branches that formed a deep well in the snow around the trunk. Deep enough for a skier to sink in, deep enough to disappear in. After the previous night's storm, some were several feet deep.

Mina stopped at the first drop of blood under a tree protected from the storm. A red streak in the snow led to more drops.

She sucked in her out-of-control breath. "No," she whispered. Proof she'd failed.

There still might be time. She pushed herself across the snow; her small amount of police training, made her careful to avoid the blood.

The red trail stopped at one tree well. A single bare hand reached out; its blue fingers barely visible through the tree branches.

Mina forgot about evidence and fumbled to kick off her skis, sinking in the snow. "Do you need help?" She knew even as she yelled it, she called out to a dead man.

As she tried to scramble through the fresh powder, she ripped the radio off her chest to call it in. "I've got a—" Mina's hand released the button.

The hand lay wholly unconnected from a body, but the depths of the tree well held something far more terrifying.

"Mina, what is it?" Sol called through the radio, which now lay on the snow.

She didn't have an answer.

Chapter 5

The body in the tree, well-hidden under the branches, was barely recognizable as human. The hand and the few other pieces left were clues enough to what it once had been. But what still remained would haunt Mina for a long time.

She wanted to run, wanted not to be the one who discovered that horror in the woods. But she wouldn't do that again. She did allow herself to rush out of the trees and call in the location. After all, there was no rescuing left to be done. The last night had been her chance, and she'd blown it.

Sol ordered her back down to the lodge, refusing to let anyone up there until the patrollers had time to set off the dynamite and any potential avalanche.

The small avalanche they did set off went straight for the ravine but avoided the trees and the body. Once the okay came to go back up, it took several tries for Mina to click back into her skis. All strength had fled from her legs; she finally used her hands to hold her knees steady as she snapped in.

On the lift ride back up, she told herself the skier had probably fallen and died. Coyotes had found the body and dragged it into the trees, abandoning the site at the approach of humans.

What did she have to be so scared of?

Mina wished she knew what drove her fears. She'd found dead bodies before; one had been attacked by coyotes before she stumbled onto it. She had to wait for two hours until a helicopter arrived to haul it out. This shouldn't feel different, but it did.

CHAPTER 5

Mina, Sol, and the full-time deputy, Clint Gallagher, skied into the site with Patrick and a few other patrollers. They all carried snowshoes attached to their backpacks.

Stopping shy of the tree grove, one rescuer next to Mina went a little off-balance, standing on only one foot, and missed his shoe. His foot hit the ground and sank into the snow almost to his waist. Mina and Patrick stood on either side of him and hefted him out.

"Should've stayed in bed, am I right? Going to be one of those days," he said, laughing as they struggled to get him back on his feet.

Mina had worked with many of these guys on and off for a few years. When she first volunteered with SAR, the joking within a few feet of a body angered her. By her second body, she teased along with them, recognizing it as a way to keep from going mad.

"Mini," one patroller yelled from further into the trees. "What are your tracks?" That was one bit of teasing she hadn't learned to embrace, Mini Mina. A nickname she'd held since childhood and had hoped would die in California. At 5'2", the name followed her everywhere. She had her Korean mother to thank for both her height and her name.

"I came in on my skis." She moved closer to the body, ignoring every instinct to flee.

"You take off your boots?"

"No, didn't want to sink in."

"Not your skis, your boots.

"Yeah." She rolled her eyes. "I took off my boots in zero degrees and walked around in the snow. Why?"

She came into a clearing where Clint stood with camera in hand, staring at the ground. The body wasn't in view quite yet; this was where she had first seen the drops of blood.

"There's a footprint here," Clint said. He had training in crime forensics that surpassed anyone else's knowledge there.

"You think the fall didn't kill him?" Mina hated to think their guy survived falling off a chairlift only to be injured and attacked by an animal.

"It looks like a bare foot."

23

"What?" She covered the last few yards in a single stride even as her snowshoes sank into the snow. She stayed in Clint's prints to not disturb the site any more than they had to.

Next to him was an indentation in the snow. She squatted down and outlined it in the air with her finger. The print showed a curve and five indents. The footprint was formed by the toe and ball only, not the heel. But the track narrowed at the ball, unlike a paw print.

She stood and scanned the area, looking for more tracks. Her own tracks from the morning were not two feet away. "Are there any others?"

"Not yet but we're still looking. I'm thinking maybe he got disorientated in the fall. Then hypothermia sets in, he gets confused, and takes his boots off."

"That doesn't make sense."

"No, but that's what hypothermia does. Makes you disorientated and feel hot."

"That's not what I meant." She squatted once again over the print. "This print wasn't here this morning, and believe me, that guy was already dead."

Sol came up to them, overhearing the last of their conversation. "How sure are you about that?"

"You can see my tracks there, but maybe I missed it." The print was alongside the drops of blood she first saw. She'd scanned the blood trail carefully and the print was deep, at least a few inches.

"Wait a second." With her palm down, she held her hand flat over the toe print. Her fingers didn't span half the print.

Sol squatted next to her, pulling out a tape measure and drawing it across the toes. They stared for a long time without speaking. His fingers hovered over each toe. "No claw marks."

Clint snapped a photo with the tape measure. "It's going to be hard to get the details in the photo. The shadows from the trees make the snow appear flat. Difficult to tell in the image how big a foot it really is."

Sol had been commander of SAR for upward twenty years. With his tracking skills, the rest of the crew joked he was the search and they were the rescue. He placed his cheek almost to the snow next to the print, analyzing it from every angle.

"What do you think?" Mina asked.

"Let's try to get a mold." Sol stood up. "Clint, keep photographing the site before dark. There's another storm coming in tonight, and we need to get everything documented and the body down."

Everyone walked off leaving Mina and Sol alone with the track. "You don't have to handle the body," Mina said. "Clint has more experience than you in crime scene analysis."

"I'm fine." Sol turned as quickly as snowshoes would allow.

Mina regretted even hinting at something she never dared mention. That other body she'd found a few years ago ravaged by coyotes had been Sol's wife, Daisy. Sol never spoke of her.

After more photographs were taken than at any wedding and a mold of the print taken, they loaded the body, or what remained of it, into a body bag.

Two ski patrollers had already puked into the trees, and Mina was determined to not join them. Her attempt to disassociate from the remains as they slid them onto a tarp failed immensely but at least her bile stayed down. There'd be plenty of time for crying and puking in her own bathroom tonight. Wouldn't be the first time.

After the patrollers left with the body, she stayed behind in the increasing darkness to place crime scene tape around the trees. She hung the tape as high as she could in case the storm dumped out. If it did snow, they'd at least be able to find the site again. December was still early in the season and the snow base would rise considerably.

After tying off the tape around the last tree, she stopped with arms still threaded through the branches. A clump of snow fell off a pine a few feet away. Silence had never been so loud. It had to be residuals from finding the body, but she couldn't get over the feeling that her movements were being tracked. Not watched, tracked.

A creak in the snow, like footsteps echoed through the woods.

Mina peered through the tree branches, seeing nothing and no one. With one last glance at the former grave, she snapped back into her skis and booked it down. As she skidded to a stop in front of the ski racks outside the lodge, Patrick came out from the ski patrol shack. "Did you hear the crappy news?"

"I found a half-eaten body today. Don't imagine there's crappier news than that." She picked her skis up and wiped the excess snow off.

"That boy who went missing, Jason. His friends called about an hour ago. Apparently, Jason turned up in the bed of a ski bunny he'd met on a lift. Told them he left a note on the truck and was sorry they didn't see it."

Mina stabbed her skis into the ground in one thrust. "You're kidding. Then who did we just haul down in a body bag?"

"Your guess is as good as mine."

Chapter 6

Mina didn't sleep, couldn't sleep.

Maybe if she'd only waited a few minutes the night before, she would've been able to save the missing skier. She should've stayed longer, gone back up, done something other than shrug her shoulders in the lodge at the advancing storm. She needed to find out what happened; she owed him that much.

With temperatures below zero outside and her apartment not much warmer, she pulled on her base layer of pants and a long-sleeved shirt while still under the covers before getting up. She was back to teaching after taking the previous day off. Usually, the thought of leading eight five-year-olds around the mountain exhausted her but now she longed to be in a more innocent world.

She stopped in the employee office to check what ability level she'd be teaching. A lone computer sat in the office with two employees lined up to check their own schedules. The first one, Jessie, a close friend of Mina's, pulled up hers. "Sweet, they changed me to off. I can drop the chutes all day long." She saw Mina standing behind her. "You in? We'll have a girls' day."

Mina stepped to the computer to check her own schedule. "Nope, I'm on Munchkins." That's what they called the four- to five-year-old classes.

"Don't hold your breath," said Callie, who had been setting the schedule for twenty years, and who everyone tried to butter up to get the good lessons. "Word's getting out about the body. All the parents are yanking their kids out of ski school."

"We just pulled it off the mountain two days ago. How does everyone know?"

"I don't know, but I got a call this morning from some New York tourists coming in for Christmas and they're already canceling."

"Sounds like we get the mountain to ourselves," said Jessie. "I'm going to change out of my uniform. You coming?"

Mina really wanted to hit the slopes and actually ski. "I've got to check with my other job," she said. Jessie lived in a house with five to ten other roommates, depending on the season. She could afford not to work for a time. But if they lost the Christmas tourists, nobody would last long. The town relied on the weeks around the holiday to make up for the fall's empty rooms.

Some of the roads had been plowed, but she still needed her Jeep's four-wheel drive to carry her down the mountain to the sheriff's office, which sat at the edge of town along the highway. To catch speeders, all they had to do was sit in their parking lot.

The building was a prefab with a metal roof to ensure the snow slid off. While it had a "cell," it was more of a windowless room that locked. It never held a criminal more than a few nights, and those criminals were usually drunks who started fights.

Besides Sol and Clint, there were two other part-time deputies across the county, which encompassed a landmass the size of Connecticut, though with a much smaller population. They had the town of Lost Gorge, nestled in a valley at 7,000 feet, and the actual county of Lost Gorge. Those three deputies worked out of the various towns in the county. None could commute up the canyon on a daily basis, especially in the winter.

Much of the saving done in the county was done on a part-time or volunteer basis. Patrick and the other ski patrollers took turns being on-call to work the few ambulances. The freeways and some highways were managed by highway patrol and state police. Emergency calls were routed to the nearest city, who would call the state police, who, if necessary, would contact Sol.

What it all added up to was a need for residents to be self-sufficient and survive long enough for help to arrive.

Mina pushed the office door open and almost turned around at the heatwave that accosted her. Clint sat at a desk inside the reception room. His tan uniform shirt hung over the back of the chair, leaving him in a white undershirt.

She immediately stripped off her parka. "What's up? You beating back winter to the tropics?"

"Heater's broke. It will only set itself to 85 degrees. I tried keeping the door propped open, but all that did was make sure it ran constantly."

"How's the body coming?"

Clint had taken several courses in crime scene analysis from the FBI, thereby becoming the county's expert. He wiped the sweat off his face. "What body? I've never seen anything like it. Far worse than—" He caught himself with a glance toward the closed door of Sol's office. "I've taken photos and poked around a bit, but it's beyond what we can do here. A courier from the FBI is picking it up for an autopsy."

Mina sank onto the folding chair in front of his desk. "Find anything that will help ID him?"

"There wasn't even a face left to know what the guy looked like, but it was a male. I pulled some prints, but nothing so far has come up in the database." His voice dropped. "Mina, that level of damage to the body was intense. It would've taken a pack of wolves or one giant grizzly to do that kind of work in one night. Some of the blood hadn't even frozen yet."

"And it's not the right time of year for a grizzly, and we haven't had a wolf in a decade." She finished. "Of course, you wake up a hibernating grizzly and all bets are off."

Sol came out of his office. "Good, you're here. I need you and Clint to canvas the town, see if anyone turned up missing." He rubbed his beard, or what little grew. Every year he attempted to grow one and every year failed. "You know the seasonal workers a lot better than either of us. A lot of them don't trust police. Talk to them and what they saw. Figure out if anyone hasn't shown up when they were expected."

"I can definitely help with that. Everybody is already talking about what happened."

Sol turned to Clint. "You focus on the tourist side of it: the hotels, the shuttles. Maybe this guy came in for a trip alone. That's why no one's missing him."

The door opened, bringing in a welcome rush of cold air and Cate Hanson, the town's newest permanent resident. She had been hired by the town council as a public relations person to revive the town's reputation after the events of last year and bring in the tourists. Tourists were a much desired and much despised group of people. Locals needed their money but resented their presence.

The town's response to Cate had been, at best, mixed. There existed a hierarchy in Lost Gorge: old residents, new residents, seasonal workers, and tourists (although the tourists didn't know that). Mina had started her residency as a seasonal worker who'd transitioned into full-time, more or less. What finally made her belong was volunteering on the search and rescue team.

"Hey, Mina," Cate said as she pulled off her coat. "What's with the heat?" That was something coming from her. Cate, a former Florida resident, wore a parka in July. Other than the freckles, her white skin looked almost translucent against her black hair.

Mina had always made an effort to be kind to Cate, remembering what it had been like to be new. "Just trying to make you comfortable."

"By the way, I took your advice and signed the kids up for ski school. Didn't want them feeling out of place."

"Good. Kids here start learning with binkies in their mouths and blankies in their hands."

Cate turned her attention to Sol. "The mayor called, and he's a little worried about what this incident might do to the Christmas season. He wants me to post an update."

Cate ran the town's social media accounts, posting and sharing outdoor photos with the tag #WhereAdventureIs. Locals used it to brag and tourists used it to plan vacations.

"Keeping the council and the mayor happy is a moving target," Sol said. Mina knew he didn't much like that part of his job. Considering the council begged him to take the spot when the previous sheriff proved far too good at keeping people happy, he had a lot of leeway to do what he wanted.

"Too late," Mina interjected. "Word is already out, and people are canceling their trips."

Cate nodded. "There are a lot of comments on Facebook. I need to post something." Sol acquiesced and took Cate into his office for an interview that Mina knew would be short on words and long on questions.

Once the door shut, Mina turned back to Clint. "How's he doing?" she said as quietly as she could without going full whisper.

"It's hard to say." Clint leaned forward in his chair. "Finding that body in the trees shook me up, and I'm not the one who had to see his own wife's body left out in the wilds."

"This was worse, much worse. What those animals did—"

"That's just it; I don't know if it was animals," Clint said. "When I examined Daisy's body, there were bite marks all over. And, despite her laying there a week before we found her, her body was in better condition than what we found today."

"What else could've done it?"

"I don't know. I only have experience with the one body ravaged by animals. The bones, though, didn't have a chew mark on them."

"But it had to be an animal," she said. "Something was in those trees."

"Something is right. Let me know if you figure out what that something was."

Chapter 7

If Mina wanted to find out who knew what, there was only one place to go—the No Name Bar.

Any random weekday; the young, single, and mostly seasonal workers in town would pack the bar. That night would be more crowded than usual with some workers' days getting canceled and everyone wanting to talk about the latest gossip. Entertainment was scarce after the sun went down.

Mina spied Patrick sitting at a table with other patrollers. She returned his wave but headed to the bar in search of people she hadn't already talked to.

Callie sat at a table with a few people Mina only knew by sight. Since moving into her own place a few seasons ago, she didn't know as many fellow employees as she once had. Callie would know everyone and where they'd been on Saturday. With it being mid-December, most tourists hadn't yet arrived.

Mina grabbed a non-alcoholic beer from the bar before squeezing through the crowds. Being on the clock as deputy meant no drinking, but she didn't want anyone else to know that.

She sat down at the table with Callie, grabbing the one empty chair.

"I don't know why the band keeps on playing," the guy sitting next to her said, struggling to carry his voice over a particularly long drum solo. "Not like anyone wants to listen to them tonight anyhow."

Mina laughed. "Not like anyone wants to listen to them most nights."

He laughed but the girl between him and Callie shot her a dirty look before returning her gaze to the drummer. Mina knew for whom the drummer tolled.

"I'm Ben," the guy said.

"Mina."

"I know. I've seen you around, but we haven't officially met before."

Mina wished it was her stunning good looks that made her so well-known, but it was just her looks that did it. She was the sole Asian instructor at the resort and only one of three in town. Growing up in Southern California, she hadn't felt 'other' that often. Here she stuck out. Guys wanted to date her because she looked like a nice complacent girl they could show off for. Once they figured out she could beat them at their own games, the interest disappeared.

"Nice to meet you," she said with a flat voice, not wanting to encourage him one way or the other until she got a better feel for him. The guitarist strummed his last note and announced a 15-minute break. The bar's collective occupants all sighed in relief except the girl, who ran to the stage to offer her compliments.

Callie leaned back with her beer. "I heard you were the one who found the poor sucker." Her voice, still used to carrying above the band, now reached the nearby tables.

Mina could hear the beer being poured as all talk stopped and eyes turned to her. "Yeah, something I won't forget." Talking about an investigation wasn't something she could do.

No one responded as they waited for her answer. "The police said I'm not really supposed to talk about it."

"Screw the police," said a voice she didn't recognize.

The whole deputy thing was a new development and most, especially if they'd arrived in town the last few weeks, wouldn't know about it yet.

"It was bad. I don't think I'm going to sleep for a while."

"I heard the head was twenty feet away from the body," someone said.

"I heard there was no head."

The conversation jumped off without much help from Mina. Most people preferred to share their own tales rather than listen to others—and Mina had come to listen.

What she wanted to know and everybody had a guess about, was the identity of the body.

Nobody had seen Steph this season, and she never missed opening day. No, someone else said, she's working in Utah, got a better offer. What about that skier someone rode the lift with, and he promised to call for a date and didn't? Or it had to be Charlie, right? More than a few people had seen him plastered by lunch and hadn't seen him since.

Mina excused herself to the bathroom to make notes on her phone of everything she'd heard. As she sat back down at the table, Patrick came over to wrestle a seat across from her. "What about the footprint?" he said in a low voice, ensuring everyone would try to listen in.

Had she been a little closer, she would've elbowed him. Sol had specifically asked that information stay private. For one reason, they didn't know for sure it was a footprint and for another, bits of information about investigations were always held back.

"What footprint?" someone asked.

He leaned closer as if telling a secret, which he was. "One single bare footprint in the snow, larger than the dead guy's foot. Larger than any guy's foot." The crowd quieted.

Onstage, the band strummed their guitars and Callie yelled out. "Shut up for once and read the crowd." A smattering of applause shut down the music.

"He's full of BS," Mina said, wanting to end the conversation. "And he's full of whiskey." Patrick, a Scotsman by blood, liked to brag he could slam whiskey until closing and ski a straight line home, which was probably true.

Patrick winked at her. "Mina saw it. Said it wasn't there when she first found the body. Whatever left the track walked around after the guy had been killed."

Mina glared across the table, willing him to shut up. It wasn't like him to trade on gossip. "There was no track," she said. "He's just peeing in your glass and calling it beer." The table laughed at that one. "Next thing he'll tell you is Bigfoot is hunting skiers."

Patrick took a swig. "Call it whatever you want but something ripped apart that body."

Silence quelled the laughter. Stares dropped to the ground. "So, was it really ripped apart, like people are saying?" Jessie asked.

It was one thing to laugh about gossip but another to mock truth. Every person at the table had ridden that lift, a few since they were children. The Lost Gorge world was a small one, and one among them was unaccounted for. Patrick's face flushed with shame instead of booze as he realized he'd crossed a line. "We don't...I mean it's too soon."

Mina stood. "They're still investigating, but it was probably an animal attack. Patrick, you want to drive me home?"

He followed her out the door as the band started playing. This time no one objected. As soon as the door shut behind them, she began her attack. "You absolute idiot. You know you're not supposed to say that. Not only are you screwing with the investigation, you're going to freak out the town."

He took a step back at her onslaught. "I'm sorry; you're right."

Her mouth hung half-open with the retort she'd been about to make.

"I drank too much," he continued.

There were two things she'd never heard Patrick say and that was 'I'm sorry' and 'I drank too much.'

"You okay?" She hadn't seen much of him since last winter when they'd made their latest attempt at dating. Each attempt had ended in the spring when they both literally went their separate ways.

"Yeah, I'm just..." He looked down at the ground. "I'm sorry for the way things ended. You deserved better than that."

She cocked her head. "Patrick, things ended exactly how I expected them to."

"It doesn't change the fact you deserve better than that, maybe we both do."

"Where you staying this season? I can drive you home."

His shoulders slumped. "Just moved in with Wes yesterday to couch surf until I figure some stuff out. He's inside; I'll catch a ride with him."

"Is Wes still hanging with Charlie," she asked, remembering the off-the-cuff comment in the bar.

"As far as I know."

"Could he have gotten drunk enough to fall off a chairlift?"

"He once got drunk enough to use a two-story house as a jump with his snowboard."

"Is that how he got that scar?"

"Yeah, we were all a pack of idiots back then." When Patrick usually talked about the dumb testosterone-fueled antics of his not-so-distant past, he did with a degree of pride. The somber note wasn't like him.

"You sure you're doing alright?"

"Yeah, I'll ask around about Charlie. He's been wandering off more since he got fired."

One thing about the crowd they ran with, was that you never could keep track of their location. The other thing was that everyone would surface in time for the Christmas rush. Their jobs, and thus their resort passes, depended on it.

He returned to the bar while she headed to her Jeep, wondering what had happened to Patrick. Maybe seeing that body had shaken up more people than her.

Chapter 8

A few states and a world away from Lost Gorge, software developer Ryan Lehman squinted at his computer screen. The windowless room kept him literally in the dark about whether the sun had set or not.

The tech company he'd worked at for the last five years was on the verge of going public. They'd scheduled to launch their next piece of software to coincide with the debut of their IPO. Ryan was tasked with making sure it went without a hitch. It never did, of course, but he was working into the night to make it as hitch-less as possible.

A year from now, if all went well, he would possess stock in the high six figures, a job that paid in the low, and could stop working 80-hour weeks.

He ignored his buzzing phone the first, second, and third times. By the fourth, he pulled it out to shut it off but caught sight of a text from a friend: *Vindication?* The friend included a link to a story on Facebook from a town called Lost Gorge. A body had been found, and the sole evidence, a single bare footprint.

A few commenters on the site asked about Sasquatches and yetis. The town's account had replied on a few threads, "you never know" with a link to an old story from the 1950s. Apparently a white-haired, man-like beast had attacked a hunter, pulling him clean out of his snowshoes.

It was nothing Ryan hadn't read about or investigated a hundred times. His few vacations and every free weekend had been dedicated to the search for Bigfoot. Buried in the comments of the post, though, someone had mentioned the condition of the body or the pieces left. Now that stood out with a familiarity Ryan longed to forget.

Twenty years had passed, but he could still smell the death. However, it was the smell of something living and watching that had kept him up many nights since.

Despite the late hour, employees still packed the building. He retreated outside, the only place where he could find some privacy.

His friend and fellow Bigfoot enthusiast, Phillip Griffith, picked up on the first ring. "Thought that would get your attention."

"What are the authorities saying?"

"Not much. It's a tourist town. Saying there's been an animal attack that gruesome or saying it's a murder doesn't come off well. Probably why they're tying it to Sasquatch, trying to get people talking about something else."

"Are you going?"

"I'm already here."

"What?"

"I wanted to spend a winter in a resort town. Figured the kids would visit me more if they could ski from my backyard. Being in town is how I found out about it so soon." Phil held the enviable position of an early retiree with money to burn. Ryan could claim neither the age nor the money. His job held him hostage.

"You need to come," Phil continued. "It's too much like what you—"

"I know what I saw. Don't jump to conclusions; that's how people start making up evidence."

Phil laughed into the phone. "Who are we if we're not jumping to conclusions? The kids are coming a few days after Christmas for a few weeks. You're welcome to stay until then."

"I can't, Phil. This couldn't have come at a worse time. I'll be doing 16-hour days all week." Ryan had been sleeping on a cot in the bullpen for the past two nights.

"See you in a few days."

"I'm not coming."

Phil laughed again as Ryan hung up the phone. He returned to his desk and tried to focus on code that now read more like gibberish. With a glance behind him, he opened the link on his third screen. He logged into a Bigfoot chat site he frequented, looking for more information on the Lost Gorge incident.

The site definitely had more information than what the article said, including a lot of speculation and outright made-up stuff. He knew enough to sort to the nuggets of truth.

A few hours went by as he read through the threads. A couple of people had stories about running into Bigfoot in that area—nothing concrete—a print here, a sound there.

Ryan downed another Red Bull as he refreshed the page. The can dropped to the floor as a new image appeared.

Anyone else wouldn't have understood what they looked at, but Ryan did. He'd seen a body torn apart like that once before.

He opened a new tab on his Internet and typed 'cheap airline tickets.'

Chapter 9

Mina passed on the little information she'd culled from the seasonal workers to Sol, who would work any leads with Clint. That left her to return to the one job she actually knew how to do. Her dry spell of no lessons hadn't lasted long. They'd assigned her a class of six-year-olds, who'd never been on skis before. A lot of the more seasoned instructors flat out refused to teach that level and that age. Mina didn't mind; bookings were still down. Plus, as fast as kids learn, she'd be taking them down chutes in a few seasons.

At the end of the day, she ushered them inside to the indoor portion of ski school. This part, which was a lot of the younger one's favorite part, included hot chocolate and a movie while they waited for their parents to trickle in.

She sat her class at a long lunch table where another class and their instructor already sipped their hot chocolate.

"We didn't see the monster," said one of Cate Hanson's twins, a towheaded boy named Chris.

"What monster?" asked one of the other kids.

"You know the monster that ate the skier."

Eyes widened. "Where at?"

"Right on a chairlift. That's probably why we didn't see it. Maybe tomorrow when teacher takes us up the lift. It's got fangs and everything."

Mina had caught the end of the conversation as she walked back to the table balancing four cups of hot chocolate. "A monster didn't eat a skier. He's telling stories." She set down the cups without dripping more hot chocolate on her already-stained ski pants.

"Nuh-uh," Chris shouted. "I heard my mom saying so."

Mina made a mental note to talk to Cate. "What was everyone's favorite part of the day?" Working with kids meant constant redirection.

"Not getting eaten by a monster," said the girl.

"No, that would've been awesome," said one of the other boys.

"Movie time," the other instructor announced, doing a better job of distraction.

They herded everyone over to the bright red bean bags in front of a TV and a DVD of *Frozen*. It didn't take long until several eyes, including the twins', drooped from the day's exertion.

It fell on the instructors to clean up the room. Mina used the quiet time to wipe down tables while the other instructor, a younger woman she couldn't quite place, picked up garbage.

"Did you enjoy the band at the bar?" the instructor asked.

Mina recognized her then as the girl enthralled with the band. Her name tag read, 'Adrienne.' She must be a first-year worker or Mina would've known her.

"They were definitely…rocking."

"So rocking."

Another memory came back. Adrienne had mentioned being stood up on a date at the bar. A glance at the kids showed they were too engrossed in the movie or exhausted to pay attention to a conversation happening twenty feet away.

"Did that guy ever call you?" Mina asked.

Adrienne paused, paper cups in hand. "What guy? Oh, from the weekend. Nope, must've been eaten by the monster."

Mina tried to laugh, not wanting to let on that's what she was wondering. "He didn't call or anything?"

"No, and I only gave him my digits so I couldn't call him. Too bad, though, I like my guys cute and from out of town. Although he was divorced and I'm not sure I want seconds yet." Adrienne looked fresh out of college.

"Where was he from?"

"I don't remember, but he worked as a reporter for some outdoor magazines. He would've been a good hook-up for swag."

Mina dumped out her rag in the nearby sink. "No kidding. Do you remember his name?"

"Why do you ask, hoping to steal him away?"

"No, I like my men from town. I've been helping the sheriff cobble together a list of who the body might be. He figured I know all the regulars." Her being deputy wasn't a secret, but it still felt uncomfortable to say it out loud, like doing so would make it more real.

"I doubt it was him. I bet he left town early. He had a red-eye flight and probably didn't want to chance the roads. His name was Jay or Gray. Something like that."

A slight knock came at the door. Cate, stood there, looking sheepish. "I'm so sorry. Work ran late."

"No worries, half the class is still here."

She strode in. "Good, I had a Zoom call that would not end." Cate carried herself with the air of a woman on the way to a board meeting, despite wearing jeans and sweaters and having dark brown hair. Mina wasn't sure why, but she pictured all high-powered executive women as wearing high heels with blonde hair. Since Mina couldn't manage either, it was good she'd walked away from the corporate world.

Whatever Cate had done in her previous life, Mina figured her to have been successful. The one time she'd asked her about it, Cate had laughed and said she ran marketing for a company that required eighty hours and her soul, and that her and the kids needed a new life.

"It's okay. Might want to warn you, though, Chris was telling the class the tale of the snow monster. Said he overheard you mentioning it."

Cate rolled her eyes. "Great, that's actually the reason I'm late. My call was with the Sasquatch Searchers of America with all sorts of questions about the beast. Apparently, they saw the article on Facebook."

"I can't believe you posted that." Sol had almost raised his voice at Cate when he'd found out about the article. Her argument that she hadn't posted anything the entire town wasn't already talking about anyhow didn't quell his ire.

Cate shrugged. "Better to have people talking about Bigfoot than murder. Whatever the situation, you can always turn it to your advantage." She glanced behind Mina to where her kids were still focused on their movie and lowered her voice. "You were there. Did you see the footprint? Was it really as big as people are saying?"

Ten years Mina had been living in this town and it wouldn't be saving lives that finally brought her notice—it would be finding Bigfoot. Adrienne, in an obviously casual way, leaned closer.

"Everyone's exaggerating it, and we can't say for sure it was even a footprint."

Cate looked disappointed. "Of course, it's just I was hoping…"

"What?"

The next words came out in a rush. "Bookings are still down and will be until we get it figured out. In the meantime, a filmmaker is coming tomorrow and staying for a few weeks to do a documentary. He'd probably love to talk to you."

"You've got to be kidding."

"We can't change what happened, but we can change the story around it."

"I'm not talking to those weirdos."

Despite her best intentions, those weirdos would talk to her.

* * *

Mina waited on a flat area in front of the lodge the next morning for her client, a tourist. She hoped this meant tourists were finding their way back.

A tall and very good-looking guy, like TV good-looking, approached her with his hand outstretched. "Mina?"

"Are you my lesson?" *Please say yes,* she thought.

"Yes, I'm Lane Jenkins."

Things were looking up. She took the proffered hand and wondered how many women had been won over by his gregarious smile. She would decide later if she'd be one of them. "What made you decide to take a ski lesson today?"

"I skied as a teenager, but it's been a few years. Thought it might be a good idea to brush up my skills my first day back."

"Let's see what you got."

What he had was the ability to turn and stop. But after he found his sea legs, he sped up, probably to impress her and himself. It would take a lot more than bombing a green run to impress her, but she appreciated the effort.

As they skidded to a stop in front of the lodge, he leaned in and nudged her with a pole. "How am I doing, Coach?"

"You're picking it up fast. You'll be ripping around the mountain by tomorrow." She didn't have to struggle to compliment this green-eyed charmer.

He bought her lunch in the lodge and over bison burgers, he glanced around the lodge and its empty chairs. "When does the busy season start? With it being the week before Christmas, I thought there'd be more crowds."

"It varies year to year."

"People aren't staying away because of that..." At her sharp glance, he adjusted his words. "...incident."

"What incident?"

"You know the..."

She waited, not offering him any opening.

He must've known his charm was down to a trickle. "They say you saw him." The smile dropped.

"They say wrong."

"They said an Asian ski instructor found the body."

Some days, it didn't pay to be one of the few minorities in town. "Even if I did, why would I talk about it with you?"

"I'm studying Sasquatch. I want to know what happened up there and so do you."

"Not good enough."

He leaned closer and grabbed her sleeve. "Because I can pay you, and I assume you need the money. I'm making a documentary."

She pushed her chair back but it caught on the carpet and snagged, tipping it over. The few patrons eating turned their attention to Mina. She swallowed the 'screw you' she wanted to say. "I'm sorry, Lane," she said with false cheer. "I won't be able to help you with that."

Before she could reach the door, he followed her and opened it for her. "We still have a half-day of lessons."

She had two choices to get out of the rest of the day—fake injury or fake sick. Both would put her at the bottom of the assignment list in an already slow winter. Last year she'd showed up to work with two broken fingers and the flu rather than lose her shot at wealthy clients.

Mina would do a lot for money, but she wouldn't bandy around someone's death like it was entertainment.

"You want to ski with me, we're going to spend the afternoon on the bunny hill working on your form and only discussing skiing. If you don't like that, we can call it a day."

The charm returned. "Sounds like a good plan to me."

Every ride up the short chairlift Mike peppered her with questions. Some about skiing, some about the body. She ignored the latter.

At the end of the day, he slipped a hundred-dollar bill into her hand. "Mina, I've got a million dollars riding on finding out what happened up there. This isn't the first time this has happened. You can help me or not, but I will find out."

She took the money and tucked it into her pocket. "I'm just a ski instructor, can't help you." But there was someone she would help.

Chapter 10

The sheriff's office door slammed behind her. Sol, who must've beat her by seconds, was taking his coat off. With one look at her, she didn't need to ask for an update. "The FBI is assuming animal attack so we're not a priority." He hung his coat up.

Mina thought of Clint's concern about the lack of teeth marks.

Sol walked into his office, and she followed. "Still no ID," he said. "They ran the DNA through their database but nothing came up—no missing persons. I've asked them to create a genetic profile." A profile could narrow down more specifically race and background. "From the remaining hand, they're assuming white male."

"Oh good, they've really narrowed it down." Mina slumped into a chair across from Sol.

"Have you found Charlie?"

"He hasn't shown up for at the resort, but according to his supervisor, that's not unheard of. I talked to a few of the people he lives with, but they couldn't say for sure what day they saw him last or even if he's staying with them. Nobody would know if he's dead or not."

Sol dropped his head. "I can't believe a man can fall that far that fast."

She cringed, forgetting momentarily that Charlie had done a short stint as a deputy under the previous sheriff. "Sorry."

Even though she and Sol lived in the same town, they lived in different worlds and hers was for more transitionary. She had a friend killed in an avalanche last year and it was two weeks before they found him, a week before anyone knew he was missing. They mourned, but everyone moved on. They were an independent bunch that separated and came back together—most of the time.

She thought of their John Doe; did anyone look for him beside them? Every time Mina closed her eyes all she saw was the hand reaching out like a drowning man.

As if sensing her thoughts, Sol said, "It'll fade in time."

No, it won't. "Do you ever get tired of bringing home only bodies?"

"Yes."

"What do you do?"

He leaned back into his chair as the clock behind him struck five. "During 9-11, the rescue dogs would get depressed at not finding any live victims. Their handlers would hide in the wreckage of the Twin Towers so the dogs could find them. Gave them a sense of accomplishment to abate the discouragement."

"Are you going to hide for me, Sol?"

"No, because you know what those dogs didn't. There will always be someone in need of saving."

"Why do I have to be the one who saves them?" She felt guilty even as she asked it.

Sol had been the only boy born in a family of four girls. His grandfather had called him Solo Vino, *He Came Alone.* There wasn't a more apt description of a man who longed to be anywhere people weren't. The sheriff job wore on him, but he never complained.

Sol held out his empty hands to show he didn't have the answer. "I don't know, but I've committed for a year, and I need people I can trust."

A year doing the same thing, not being able to take off on a long trip or do her own thing? Granted, she had a job most of the time to pay the bills but each one only lasted for a few months. In between seasons, she lost herself in the void. Her gut clenched at the thought of being held in place. "I don't know if I could say yes to that."

"How about two months? Can you commit for two months? Then you can decide for good at the end of it."

If there was anything Mina excelled at, it was procrastinating life decisions.

During college, she'd had her entire career mapped out for her, but the recession pissed on those plans, for which she was eternally grateful. She refused to be trapped again. "Why two months?"

"Clint would like to be able to take a few weeks off when the baby comes. And I don't think he'd mind not being on call as often for the first few months."

"Full-time? I've got another job, you know. I've been booked over all the holidays." If everyone didn't cancel.

"I know, but if Clint knows he'll be off when the baby comes, I can convince him to work the holidays."

Outside the wind blew and nearby tree branches scraped against the metal roof. Another storm was coming. She had loved that sound and what it promised. Since the body, though, storms kept her on edge.

"Mina, we need your help to figure out what happened to the skier."

She turned away from the window. "Okay, two months, tops. I've got a lot of clients coming in March."

Mina needed to know what happened to the skier as well.

Chapter 11

Ryan stood on the curb of an airport small enough to have only one security guard. The winds tossed around a few pieces of sagebrush and old snow across the flat plains. He unconsciously gripped the strap of his large backpack a little tighter, grateful to have shoved in all his winter clothes.

Phil pulled up in a Range Rover, and Ryan jumped in. "Where are these mountains you've been bragging about?"

"They're more impressive, the closer you get." Phil pointed to some distant hills. "It's a two-hour drive just to get to the base."

"Learn anything more?" Ryan asked.

Phil turned down a radio station that had equal amounts of static and music. "I talked to one of the guys on ski patrol. It was bad enough he quit his job the next day. Said whatever did that was straight-up evil."

Ryan remembered that feeling well.

"Snow's covered the site a few feet over. Plus, it's on ski resort land, making it difficult to do any kind of investigation," Phil said.

Ryan removed his outer jacket at the flow of heat. "What's the history of the area?"

"Sasquatch-wise? Not much. Summer would be a lot better for hunting. I've tried to talk to a few of the old-timers, but they'd never admit seeing him even if they'd sat across from the beast. A small town doesn't allow for being too far off the normal line."

"Well, you're in for a long winter," Ryan said.

Phil laughed. "They're not much for outsiders either. Don't blame

49

them; I'm not worth the trouble. One guy, though, mentioned some odd experiences but then one of his brothers walked up…Hold up." He punched the volume up on the radio.

"…you need to go and stay there," a weatherman said. "The mountains are in for a three-day dump. The timing of the storm…" The radio receded into static.

Phil punched the gas a little harder. "Used my four-wheel-drive more in the last week than all of last year. How'd you swing work?"

"I told them I had a family emergency, then stayed up all night trying to get everything done." Ryan pushed down the guilt. After five years of giving everything, he could take a few days. Only the promise he'd be connected to Wi-Fi to handle all the bugs kept them from firing him.

"Eighty hours a week isn't worth it no matter the pay."

"Says the tech CEO, who is now retired before fifty."

"Retired, but I worked my youth away. I kept thinking my payday was just around the corner. Then I went around the corner and my kids were grown and gone. You could stand to find someone besides me to have an adventure with. Don't wake up ten years from now alone and wealthy."

"I won't." Ryan had his doubts about that but didn't want to disappoint one of his only friends.

The snow started by the time they reached the Junction, the last gas station, according to Phil, before the climb up the canyon.

"We'll be out of the canyon before the real snow comes," Phil said as he filled up the tank.

"Want me to drive?" Phil's past life as CEO hadn't given him much winter driving experience. The car was a new one.

"Go for it," he said, tossing Ryan his keys. "I've got no ego wrapped up in my driving."

Within a few hundred yards of the canyon's steep cliffs, the snow stuck to the roads and the double yellow lines vanished.

About halfway up, he hit a white wall of blowing snow coating the black pavement and everything else. The snowflakes filled the headlights, making driving with or without light equally perilous. Despite the four-wheel drive, the tires slipped in the snow. He eased off his gas pedal, allowing the car to slow on its own volition. Hitting brakes on roads like these would mean a skid.

"I've never seen anything like this," Phil whispered, as if speaking out loud would disrupt Ryan's focus.

As the highway steepened, the tires slipped again. There was no going back down as that would be even slicker. If he missed a turn, they'd end up a hundred feet down in a river.

With no other choice, he crossed the white line, or what should be the white line if he could see. He pulled off to the shoulder, maybe. "I can't see the edge of the road."

Phil shook his head. "I can't see past the car."

Ryan pushed open the door and stepped out into six inches of powder. With his foot, he dug into the snow until he reached dirt. At least he hadn't parked on the road. "We can wait here and see if a plow goes by and follow it up."

As he turned off the engine to preserve gas, the oppressive silence barged in. Only then could he appreciate their predicament and fool-heartedness.

"What if they close the canyon?" Ryan said. "I read somewhere the pass closes occasionally due to avalanches. There may not be a plow coming."

Phil leaned over the console to check the odometer. "I set this before I left. We're only a few miles from the top."

"A few miles of road we can't see. Let's give it a few minutes and see if any cars come by."

Ryan turned on the engine after wiping the snow from the exhaust pipe. No sense in adding carbon monoxide poisoning to the situation. In the few minutes it had been off, the car's interior had already dropped to 35 degrees.

Chapter 12

Mina's phone rang as she pulled out of the parking lot. "Hey, you off work?" Her friend Jessie asked as a hello.

"Yeah, did you want to grab something to eat?"

"No, I want your Jeep. I'm stuck in a snowdrift and could use your winch."

Many a day Mina regretted buying a car with the ability to tow others. "Where are you?"

"Not that far, only the Junction."

Mina checked the weather on her app. "It's supposed to snow. Just spend the night with Casey." Casey was her on and off and on boyfriend.

"I can't. I've got clients already in town. I'm supposed to meet them in the morning. If the storm hits like they're saying, I won't make it. If they get another instructor, I'm out $500."

A few stars already appeared in the western sky, meaning the storm held off. It was about a thirty-minute drive to the Junction. They could leave Jessie's car and return for it after the storm. Still, Mina hesitated, the southern winds blew hard. The air hummed with anticipation.

"I'm coming now." Mina should've known better, but she hit the gas down the canyon as the first snowflakes fell.

A half-hour later, Mina cursed Jessie for her own stupidity. How many times had she watched the skies change in an instant? As Mina's Jeep crept down the canyon, she muttered, "Flurries, this ain't." She once bragged to a tourist who'd paid her $250 to drive him to the airport during a particularly bad snowstorm that she could drive this canyon blindfolded.

She was wrong. Never had Mina seen a storm descend with such speed and fury. Black roads turned white before her mind registered it was snowing.

Her beams highlighted each flake, making it seem like she drove in a snow globe. Only the needle of her speedometer, hovering below 10, proved she moved at all.

The snow tires and studs she'd spent a paycheck on gripped the road, and she felt no fear about a potential slide-off. Driving over a cliff in blinding snow, however, kept her body completely tense and leaning forward in her seat as if that would help her see better.

A few miles down she relinquished all hope of making it to the Junction. All she needed now was a place wide enough to turn around.

She passed a sign that read *View Area Ahead,* or at least it did in the summer. Now all that showed through was *View* and the *d.* She would've slowed, but any slower and she'd be stopped. Twenty more yards and she could turn.

The white expanse opened up, and she cranked her wheel to the left. Mina didn't see the other car until she hit it. Or at her speed, nudge might be the more appropriate word. She unclenched her toes

A gangly man crawled out of the front seat and another guy out of the passenger as she waved with a sheepish smile.

The second Mina opened the car door, her beanie almost blew off her head. She caught it and shoved it down over her ears. She met the men where their bumpers touched.

"Sorry," she said by way of introduction.

The driver glanced down at her. "I'm sorry, I didn't realize how close I was to the road."

"What road?" Her tracks were already filling with snow.

"It's no problem," the passenger said. "I knew living here would be hard on a car."

"You live here?" Mina asked, eyeing him. His clothes were too new and unworn to be a local, too nice to be a seasonal worker, but not expensive or old enough to be a "second home for the winter" person.

"I rented a house for the winter."

She would have to recalculate her assumptions about strangers. "Welcome, I'm Mina Park."

He was average size with an age hard to pin down, maybe forty, maybe older. "Philip Griffith. This is my buddy Ryan Lehman, just picked him up from the airport."

Mina reached out a hand, which he shook without making eye contact. She wondered how, with his barely-there width and length stretching to the sky, he managed to stay tethered to the ground. "Nice to meet you."

He mumbled something in return. It drove her nuts how weird guys can be about women, as if they were an alien race bent on world domination. At least the alien part was untrue.

"Are you stuck?" she asked Phillip, deciding to ignore the tall one.

"Not so much stuck, as blind. Hoping the wind will die down so we can keep going up." He stuck his bare hands into his pockets. "What about you?"

"I was heading down but gave up. If you want, you can follow me up the canyon. Sometimes it helps to have a pair of taillights to chase."

Ryan glanced back to the road and back to her, apparently debating. "I don't know," he said to Philip. "Maybe we should wait for a plow to go by and follow it up. What do you think?"

She didn't respond, assuming he spoke to his friend. Both men looked to her for an answer. "Probably the smartest thing to do," she said after a moment's hesitation.

"Probably?" Phil asked.

"If visibility gets too bad, the plows won't be out, and you risk the roads being closed. The later it gets, the worse the storm is supposed to be." The snow blew around them like it did the evening she should've found the skier.

She stomped feeling back into her feet, anxious to be on the road. She despised this feeling of unsafe. This was her world, her place. She should be able to handle a stupid storm.

"I'm going up," she said with no idea if that was the brave or cowardly thing to do. "You want to follow me, you can."

Mina didn't wait for an answer before climbing back into the Jeep. As she backed off the other bumper and pulled into what she hoped was the road, their headlights flipped on and they pulled out behind her.

Chapter 13

Ryan knew the silence wouldn't last long but still cringed when Phil broke it. "I like her."

"She's probably not single."

"You don't know that for sure. If I were you, I'd be finding out."

"Anyone else coming for the hunt?" Ryan ignored the perpetual yenta.

"Plenty of folks. It's close to Christmas break, and people have the time off work."

"For those poor suckers who work." Ryan tried not to expend too much jealousy on his friend. Phil's wife had died right before, and he suspected his friend would willingly trade the money to get her back. He also suspected the loneliness was what drove much of his friend's matchmaking.

Once they pulled back onto the highway, Ryan halted all conversation to focus on the taillights ahead. It was all he could do to not let the woman on the roadside hear his fear. He'd slept alone in the Montana woods with wolves howling and something unknown rustling in the trees that he'd half-hoped was a bear. But driving on these roads was something else.

With no sense of distance or time, he followed until Mina's right red light blinked. He relinquished his grip slightly. Were they there? She pulled off and parked in a small pull-out, not unlike where they'd been stopped earlier.

As he put the car into park, the adrenaline that had been coursing through his body flowed out. The muscles in his arms felt like he'd been lifting weights for an hour.

"Why'd we stop?" Phil asked.

The answer to his question lay before them under eight inches of snow:

a small Audi, which should be sitting in a garage, not going up a mountain pass. A man climbed out of the car as they and Mina got out of theirs.

"...wanted to get up before the storm. Thought I had time," the man said as they approached. He wore a ski jacket that Ryan had seen online for an easy grand when he'd been outfitting himself for the season. Ryan went with something less, well less everything.

"We all did," the woman replied. "I'm Mina." She stuck her hand out to shake.

"James."

"I'm Phil. This is my friend, Ryan." He nodded in Ryan's general direction, and he nodded back, content to stay in the background.

"Sorry," Mina said. Ryan glanced around before realizing she addressed him. "I shouldn't have had you follow me in the car. These roads are..."

"We tried." There weren't words to describe how bad things had gotten. The snow was so deep, the grill on her Jeep skimmed it.

A lone streetlight powered by solar lit up the pullout. "I've been sitting here for an hour and can't go any further in my car," James said. He flashed a smile at Mina that communicated 'I can convince you to do anything.' "Would you mind if rode up with you? My wife and kids are up there already, hate to make them worry."

"Is your family on vacation?" Mina asked.

"No, my wife, Cate, got a job working for the town."

Mina visibly relaxed. "I know your twins. I've been teaching them to ski."

"I'm sorry."

She laughed. "No, they're learning fast, surprising considering they haven't had much experience with snow."

"It's in their—"

"Not to interrupt," Ryan said, "but those roads aren't getting any better." His hands, despite the gloves he wore, tingled in the cold.

Mina looked at him as if appraising him. "You're right." All levity dropped from her voice, and he felt a slight pang of guilt. "But I think we ought to wait it out, see if the storm clears out or a plow comes through."

James took a step forward. "If you're nervous about driving, I'm more than happy to drive your Jeep."

Mina's glare dropped about twenty degrees, and Ryan was quite pleased with himself for not being dumb enough to say that. "I can drive my own car."

"What about you?" James asked Ryan. "Your ride looks like it's got four-wheel drive."

"If she says it's better to wait it out, I'm inclined to agree."

Mina shot him a look he couldn't quite read. Not being able to read people wasn't anything new to him.

"I've got $500 if you can get me up there tonight," James said. "I really hate that my family is in this storm by themselves."

"$500 wouldn't pay for my funeral," Mina said. "And I know Cate; I think she'd rather have a live husband than a dead one."

"You'd be surprised," he muttered before climbing back into his car. Mina turned to her own Jeep, leaving Ryan and Phil standing in the snow.

"Let's see what we've got in the car to wait this out," Phil said.

The snow was already to the tailpipe so there'd be no running the engine. Phil rummaged through the back while Ryan pulled out his suitcase from the backseat and unzipped it to reveal enough warm clothes to cover him three times over. He split them with Phil.

Ryan pulled on his new snow boots, rated to zero degrees. If he had wood, he would've knocked on it to make sure he wouldn't have to test that.

"Come get in," Mina yelled from her Jeep

With a lift on her Jeep, her tailpipe was out of the snow and the engine running.

Ryan moved to climb into the backseat but Phil beat him to it, gesturing to the front. "You take that, you're taller."

He should've used that height to kick Phil on his match-making shins.

Settled in, they all sat in silence for a moment watching it snow. "We may be here a while," she said. "I've seen this canyon close for a couple of days."

"How far are we from the top?" Phil asked.

"A mile, maybe more. Do you have any food?"

"A bag of jerky. You?"

"A 72-hour kit with food and water…"

"Great."

"…that's several years old."

Despite their situation, he couldn't help but laugh. "Water might still be good."

James knocked on the window. "Mind if I get in?"

They settled in with Mina passing around a few water bottles she happened to have, and no one mentioning the hunger pains their stomachs announced.

Within an hour, the snow covered the exhaust pipe, and they turned the engine off.

Chapter 14

The snow never stopped falling. The cold became a part of Mina, interwoven into every atom of her body.

The men had retreated into themselves and it fell on her to strike up some conversation to pass the night. "James, Cate said you were working out of the country, but she didn't say where."

"Did she?" He shuffled around in the backseat until his head popped through the seats. "I'm a consultant so I'm constantly moving around. Some mornings I turn on the TV just to see what language they're speaking."

"Can't be easy with a family."

"No, but I'm taking a bit of a sabbatical. We moved to Lost Gorge as a break from the rat race."

"It's not permanent?" Cate had told Mina she wanted to make Lost Gorge home.

"Maybe a year or so. Cate likes to think longer but my career won't allow it." He moved his attention back to Phil who'd curled up in the corner. "What about you? In for the winter?"

Phil hadn't said much since meeting James on the roadside. "Yeah, my kids are all in college, and I didn't want to live in an empty nest."

"You retired?"

Phil hesitated a moment, like he'd fallen asleep before offering a quiet, "Yes."

"Congrats, on being early. No way you're 65."

Mina, who would be paying off student loans until 65, swallowed the jealousy or tried to. "What about you?" she said to Ryan. "You retired as well?"

"No, I'm a software developer. This is the first week off I've had in several months."

"What brought you up? The snow?" Mina didn't remember seeing skis on his roof or poking through the seats.

"Yeah." He glanced to the backseat. "Phil said it would be awesome skiing." Funny, he didn't strike her as a skier.

The streetlight maintained its vigilance through the night as they tried and failed to sleep. A coyote howled, and she wondered why it ventured out in the storm.

"Is that what people are saying killed the skier, a coyote?" James asked.

"Didn't you hear, it was Bigfoot," Mina said with an edge in her voice.

"Did they find any tracks?" Ryan asked.

"Nothing definite." She decided it was time for a change of subject. "What do you do for a living that keeps you on the road so much?" She asked James. "Roadie with a rock and roll band?"

"No, I'm a straight-up groupie." He said it in such a deadpan way, it took her a second to get the joke.

She chuckled. "That can't pay well."

"It's more about the perks than the money. No, I'm kidding; I'm a business consultant. I specialize in transportation improvements, which means I spend way too much time in India."

"It must be hard to be gone so much," Ryan said.

He said this as Mina offered an opposing opinion. "How fun, traveling all over the world. I spent a month in India a few years ago. What cites were you in?"

"It is hard, and the most of any city I saw was the inside of an office or a hotel so I'm fairly unfamiliar with the country." James took a deep but ragged breath.

She turned around in the seat. His brow glowed with sweat in the soft glow of the streetlight. "Hey, you okay?" Took a moment of fumbling to find the cargo light before she could switch it on.

James's face had paled in the last few hours and sweat slicked back his hair.

"I'm okay."

"You can't be hot." Her words appeared as clouds in front of her.

Ryan turned in his seat. "You sick?"

"No, I have…" He took a breath. "…I have a heart condition. I ran out of pills, but I figured I could fill a prescription when I got up there. I can usually skip a day without it affecting me too much."

"How long has it been?"

"Tomorrow morning or I guess today will be two days?" His statement sounded more like a question. "I got caught up in work, trying to clear things out. It's no big deal; I'll take it when we get up there."

"What happens if you don't?" Mina didn't like how quickly he'd changed in a few hours.

"My heart rate goes up, and I get lightheaded." He paused. "Look it's nothing that hasn't happened before. I can handle it."

"But it could lead to a heart attack?" Ryan asked.

"Worst-case scenario, yes. But we're a long way from there." Sleep is probably the best thing right now.

* * *

Mina awoke at the first hint of dawn struggling through the storm—a light she sensed more than saw. A foot of snow covered the hood, and the side windows were plastered with ice.

Ryan stirred when she did and both their glances went to James in the backseat. He'd fallen asleep across the backseat, leaning against Phil, who sat wide awake. "A few times, I swear he stopped breathing," Phil said.

"James," Ryan asked. "How you doing?"

Without opening his eyes, he whispered. "Just peachy."

Mina pulled out her phone, which refused to turn on in the cold. It took taking off two gloves and pulling back the sleeves of four layers until she could read the time on her watch—7:22.

Ryan tried to open the door, but it had frozen shut during the night. Mina yanked on her door handle, releasing the latch. With a twist in the seat, she positioned both feet against the door and kicked. Nothing budged.

She kicked again, still nothing.

Ryan stopped her mid-kick with a hand on her shoulder. "Let me." He unhinged his long legs from their cramped position and stretched them across her lap. One kick broke the ice coating the crack; the next kick pushed the door a few inches into the snow.

The snow measured in feet. "I've got a shovel in the back," Mina said.

Phil rummaged through her stuff and pulled it out, passing it to her.

It had a sharp end on it Mina used like a pick. With several jabs, she managed to push open the door enough to reach her head out. "Crap."

"That bad?" Phil asked.

The road, or what had been the road, looked more like a snow-covered field. Drifts formed like waves and even the trees had bowed down to the power of the storm. A cracking sound broke through the still as somewhere a branch broke under the weight.

And the snow still fell, not at the same fury but still at a never-ending pace.

"It's worse. The road can be accessible by snowmobiles, but it will take at least a day until a plow manages to get this far."

She pulled the door shut to conserve what little heat the four of them generated. "James." He mumbled an indiscernible reply. "James," she said louder, demanding a response.

"What?" He said in more of an annoyed tone versus sick, making her feel a little better.

"What's going to happen if you don't get some medication soon?"

"Probably nothing as long as I take it easy. I've missed a few days before." All of this was said in a low voice without opening his eyes.

"You don't look like 'probably nothing.'"

"Cold's is making it worse than usual. When will the plow come?"

"Might be a few hours," Ryan said.

"Hopefully, they got food."

Mina ran through a mental inventory of what was in the car. It wasn't a long list when it came to things like food.

James fell back asleep as if the effort of staying awake had been too much.

He may say he was fine, but she didn't believe it. They were at 8,000 feet, which meant lower oxygen levels and more strain on the heart.

"I'm thinking about walking out," she whispered to Ryan. "I've seen this canyon shut down for two days before and this storm is something else."

"How will that help James if they can't get a plow down?"

"They can bring snowmobiles and pull him out on a sled or even borrow a Cat track from the resort. I don't need to get all the way to town. Once I get out of the canyon, I can radio the sheriff's office. We could have him out in half a day."

"I should go," Ryan said. "The drifts will be over your head one step out of the car."

"I've got a couple of pairs of snowshoes in the back."

"A couple, meaning two pairs?"

"Yeah, I always keep an extra set if a friend joins me."

Ryan glanced back to where James softly snored. "Good, I'm coming with you."

"No, you should stay here."

"And do what? Eat more food, drink more water? Phil can stay. Out there, you could get stuck in a drift and would need someone to pull you out. You can't save him if you get hurt."

Mina weighed all their options, and each came up lacking. She'd much rather go now than wait for James to have a heart attack. And two of them going would be safer than one.

Still a mile to the top. "All right," she said. "Let's go."

Chapter 15

M ina would've brought different clothes had she known she'd be hiking through four feet of snow, some of which drifted high enough to cover her head.

Despite the ever-falling snow, at least it would be easy to find their way through the canyon. The mountains on their right and the river on the left marked the path home. They walked in uncomfortable silence only to be broken by one of them, usually her having sunk through the drifts and having to climb out, much to her annoyance.

"Where are you from?" he asked after helping her out, apparently done with the silence.

"What makes you think I'm not from here?" Mina hated that question because when she replied California, they didn't like that answer. They wanted a foreign country of origin.

"Sorry, seems like in every resort town everyone is from somewhere else." She would give him that. "I'm from Pasadena."

"No way. I'm also sort of a California boy. My parents are in Oakland."

"Sort of?"

"When I was little, they moved around a lot to climb the corporate ladder. Eventually, like everyone else, they got jobs in Silicon Valley."

"What about you? Where do you live now?"

"Outside Seattle." The clouds lifted enough to allow them a view of the canyon walls. "Where'd you go to school?"

She hated this question almost as much as the 'where are you from.' "Stanford," she spat out, as if she expected him to argue with her. Two reasons brought out the terse response—one, people didn't believe a ski instructor could go to Stanford, and two, she really wished she hadn't.

"That's cool. My folks wanted me to go there, but I didn't get in." He said this without a trace of wounded pride. "My grades weren't that good."

Her grades were that good and better. Her parents saw to that—a lot of good it did any of them. "Stanford is overrated." She softened her tone because her issues weren't his fault. "Although I was on the ski team so it wasn't a total waste."

Ryan paused to pull out a small set of binoculars. He scanned the ridgeline.

"There's nothing up there," Mina said. "Only a few biking trails and an old road, but nothing passable in the winter."

"Just getting a feel for where we are. With the road being covered, this place is as remote as the tundra. Hard to remember a few days ago I sat in a coffee shop crammed with a hundred people in a city of more than a half-million. It's unnerving."

"Last time I went to LA, I thought I was going to crawl out of my skin sitting in traffic. Yet, I grew up there and thought nothing of it back then." Her gaze followed his to the ridgeline and the thought of what unseen entity could be watching them. The enormity of how stranded they really were crashed through.

Leaving the car had meant leaving their last grasp to civilization.

"Let's keep moving," Mina said. It wasn't only the isolation pushing her onward. Since that day in the trees, she'd been on edge. Something had been in that grove barely out of sight.

The cold couldn't be beaten back. It immersed itself into her boots; the foot warmer she'd put in the night before had long worn off. With every step, she squeezed her fist and opened it to keep circulation flowing.

With the cold came the opposite problem of the heat. Working through the snow worked up a sweat on her torso, which could freeze. Usually when she went snowshoeing, she wore a series of thin layers that could be removed as needed. All she'd had in her car, however, was her thickest winter coat and snow pants. Neither of which she could shed without freezing.

Less than a mile more, she told herself. Although the drifts made it feel like ten.

Ryan and his long legs led the way through the snow, making a trail she tried to follow. But his longer stride required her to take a step in between his. He paused as the wind picked up. Ahead lay the canyon and to their right a small four-wheel road leading into a side canyon.

"Anything up there?" Ryan asked.

"No, it only leads to an old mine and some trails."

He unzipped the top of his jacket. "How is it possible to be so hot and cold at the same time?"

"We shouldn't stop for long. Our sweat can start to freeze."

He nodded his agreement as he reached into his jacket pocket. "I just remembered last time I was out hiking in the winter I stuck a couple of hand warmers in my coat. But I don't remember if I used them or not." He took off his gloves, revealing bright red hands to fumble around in several pockets.

He challenged her initial opinion of him not being the outdoorsy kind. He still seemed like a walking contradiction, but so was she. Outside of Lost Gorge nobody looked at her race and size and thought, *there's an expert skier.*

Every time the resort assigned her men skiers to teach, she had to spend the morning kicking their asses so they'd spend the afternoon following hers.

"I got it."

Mina jerked with guilt as if he'd read her thoughts. Ryan held out a package with a pair of hand warmers. "Sorry, I guess I zoned out." She shook her head to dispel thoughts that wouldn't leave so easily. "Good, your hands could use them."

"Here, you take them. I'm okay."

"No."

As if sensing an unwinnable argument, he ripped open the package and handed one little white pack of warmth to her. "I'll take one; you take one."

"Thank you." She took the warmer and shook it; they required a little air to warm up. She tucked it into her mitten and wrapped her hand around it, willing it to heat up quicker.

As he mimicked her same actions, he gestured to the side canyon.

"Intriguing place isn't it. It looks like ten feet in and you lose the light and a hundred years. Places like that always keep me on my toes. That realization you really don't know what's out there."

"Where have you seen places like this?"

"I got lost once in a cave in Montana. No phone service, just a dying flashlight. I wandered for hours. Every breath resulted in nothing but coughing. Figured that was it and no one would find my body; my parents would never know what happened to me."

"What did happen?"

He laughed at the obvious question. "I got out and stayed out of caves since."

"Can't imagine that's hard to do."

"You'd be surprised how much that comes up in my life. What about you? You often find yourself wandering through a blizzard in the forest?"

"More often than you'd think. At least I have company this time."

"You didn't last time?"

"I found the body, the one everyone's talking about." Mina hadn't spoken to anyone about the day, beyond the logistics of solving the death. She didn't want to appear weak in front of Sol and Clint, didn't want to worry her parents, and couldn't talk about it in town.

He stopped, one snowshoe lifted in the air long enough she noticed. He replaced it without turning around. "That must've been awful. I'm sorry."

"No, it's me who's sorry." She stomped into the snow. "I've been on edge since it happened."

"You found a body. Anybody would be freaked."

"I've found bodies before. This was different."

"Bodies, as in plural? And you think I'm weird for frequenting caves."

She laughed, which she hadn't done much in the last week. "I volunteer with search and rescue."

"That's awesome, saving people like that."

"Not everyone."

As if sensing her discomfort, he changed the subject. "How far away is the ski resort?"

She jumped on the change. "Not far as the crow flies. If we were on top, you could see the runs. After the next bend, the road straightens out for less than a quarter-mile as the canyon flattens. I should be able to get someone on the radio soon."

Ryan clapped his hands together. "I'm buying you the biggest steak this town has once we get out of…"

They stepped around the bend. An avalanche filled the road, the snow still sliding into the river below.

It wasn't the storm that kept the plows away.

Chapter 16

Ryan hated winter. Hadn't before, but now he wanted nothing so much as a day in hell to finally warm up.

A few tree limbs and a lot more rocks and bushes littered the avalanche field. The snow slide filled the road at more than a 90-degree angle.

Next to him, Mina sighed as she stared at the obstacle. He couldn't really complain when she didn't respond with more than a sigh, could he?

He waited for Mina to speak, and he waited a while. She pulled out a radio and called out through the static to no response. Wrenching the button on top around to several different channels didn't help either.

"I don't know how long this goes or how sturdy it even is to walk on," Mina finally said.

"Think they'll send a plow up from the Junction?"

"Not as long as there's avalanche danger." Mina's voice faltered, and Ryan inwardly begged her to keep it together. He knew he could hang on if she did. "I can go back to that side canyon. There's a trail to the top of the ridge where maybe I can get a signal."

Ryan pulled off his glove and switched the hand warmer from one hand to the other. Pain struck each finger as numbness met heat. "Least we can do is reach the old prospector cabin. Isn't that close to the top?"

"You're not going," Mina said. "It's not safe, and I can't be responsible if something happens to you. This is my job, not yours."

"Mina, the math hasn't changed. You, alone, can't do it. Me, alone, can't do it. James and Phil back in the car can't go anywhere." He turned and

69

followed his tracks back down the canyon.

What weak daylight they had in the canyon faded in the ravine under a tunnel of barren trees. The snow was shallower there, where the trees blocked the storm. Branches broken by the weight of the snow crisscrossed their path. If it weren't for the trail's steepness, the going would be easier than the road.

Despite his height, Ryan huffed more than Mina. It would take time for his lungs and heart to adjust to the elevation.

The trail grew darker the farther into the ravine they walked. Ryan stopped to catch his breath, collapsing on a nearby log. As casually as he could he asked the question he'd been wanting to ask since he'd found out who she was. "What was the body like when you found it?"

He knew it was an awful question, knew she probably wouldn't answer it, but he needed to know. Their conversation came to a stop like a car hitting a brick wall.

She faced him with all five-feet-nothing, and he took a step back. "Why are you here? Only a powder hound would risk coming up the canyon in those conditions. But you haven't asked me anything about the resort—not the best powder stashes, not even where the best beer is. The only other people new to town are the…" Mina looked up at him. "You're one of them?"

"One of who?"

"Those idiot Bigfoot guys who call themselves Squatchers."

"I am not an idiot," Ryan said quietly. It exhausted him having to defend himself from everyone who made assumptions about him.

"No, you just travel across the country searching mythical creatures. With it being close to Christmas, I'm surprised Santa Claus isn't more on your radar."

"You don't know me." Ryan passed her to walk up the trail with her insults at his back. Her vehemence caught him off guard. He was used to ridicule but not anger.

"Those jerks, one in particular, has been chasing me down all week, won't leave me alone. 'Did it rip the head off? How big was it? Did you run?'" Mina paused and he turned to face her, unprepared for the betrayal in her dark eyes. "You came with me, not to help, but to pump me for information."

Her accusations hurt more than the taunts of those who mocked him. "I don't tell people because they think I'm crazy." He took a step toward her. "I swear I left the car to help you."

"You are so considerate." Water dripped down Mina's cheeks from her snow-soaked beanie and off the ends of her black braids. He wanted to brush them away but knew that would be the way to a butt-kicking.

"My parents sent me to summer camp when I was a kid. But when I came home with stories I saw a wild ape-man, they sent me to a psychiatrist and then to live at an uncle's home. He wouldn't let me online or watch TV, even confiscated my gaming system because it had "fantasy creatures" in it." Ryan met Mina's glare. "I was fourteen, and I learned not to tell people what I saw."

"I didn't see Bigfoot."

"Maybe not, but you saw something that's got you on edge."

"We're almost to the top," Mina said, passing him on the trail.

They climbed in silence. Yet another woman scared off by his "hobby," and Phil wondered why Ryan had stopped trying. Most could accept he believed in Sasquatch, a few less understood a trip in the mountains to look for one, but none could get past his absolute conviction he'd seen one.

Ryan gave up on gaining Mina's forgiveness to focus on a more immediate problem. He could still wiggle his fingers, but his toes had the flexibility of a brick and no feeling. The boots he wore, while proving waterproof, were new and stiff.

The trail crested on top of a ridge, revealing the canyon's edge and back down to the river. The peaks that should surround them on all sides still lay buried in the gray clouds. They stood for a moment, both breathless and speechless.

Mina pulled out her radio and turned it on to static. "This is Deputy Park in need of assistance." Deputy? That was new information. No one responded. A red light flashed on top. "Battery's low," Mina said.

She took off to a clearing in the thinning pine trees. Another attempt and static.

71

"Maybe we should turn it off. Give it a try when the storm clears out some," Ryan said.

"Storm's socked in. It's not clearing out today."

A break in static interrupted their debate and a man's voice broke through. "Mina, that you?"

"Yeah. I'm stranded in Lost Gorge Canyon with three tourists, one has a heart condition."

No answer. "Sol?"

"We've got two avalanches. You're going to be stranded for a while."

Chapter 17

Ryan and Mina huddled in the old mining shack for warmth. With holes between slats of wood, the cabin kept them only marginally more sheltered from the storm.

He'd lost feeling in both feet but hadn't communicated that to Mina. Rescue was a long way out, and there was nothing she could do about it anyway.

Sol told them to stay put and they would attempt to send snowmobiles along the ridge to them. As the crow flew, Mina explained, they weren't far from the ski resort. The terrain, however, with its deep ravines and rock, forced a longer route.

"I never thought I'd hate the snow," Mina said in utter disgust.

"Spoken like a true SoCal." Ryan sat on a log someone had dragged into the cabin. "A few inches and you people freak out. We Northern Californians know how to handle snow."

She side-eyed him for a second as if to gauge his intent before laughing. "True, four feet and I am undone." She stood and paced. "We should keep moving."

"I'm not leaving the cabin."

"No, I mean pace the floor. We sit; we fall asleep and that's death."

He thought of the last time he'd been close to death. He'd done the opposite and held perfectly still and lived. He still climbed to his feet to follow her advice.

"How'd you get from Stanford to here?" he asked, wanting to get her talking about something that wouldn't make her mad at him.

She flinched at the question, and he realized that wasn't the subject to do it. "I graduated pre-law during the recession, 100K in debt. I could go to law school and double that, but the lawyers I knew graduating were either working as waitresses or making under 40 grand as lawyers."

"Not the life everyone promised, was it?"

Mina stopped her incessant pacing and took a seat on the log next to him. "I work two jobs at a time, four or five in the year," she said resignedly. "I still owe 60K on a worthless degree. I've watched countless kids over the years come here for a season after college, swearing they'll never be like their parents. Then they get tired of living with ten people and go back."

"And you think they gave up?"

"Everybody would say they grew up." She took off her mittens and blew into her hands. "Sometimes I wonder if it isn't time for me to grow up as well."

"I'm grown up and I work twelve-hour days. I live for the weekend and the chance to have miles between me and civilization. We all do the best we can."

With a wry smile that didn't reach her eyes, she stood. "They ought to be here soon, but we need to stay warm and awake."

He tried to stand but a sharp pain shot through his leg and out his teeth. He groaned as he collapsed back down.

"What is it?" Mina asked.

"My feet." He let out a breath in hopes he could let the pain out with it. He didn't. "They've been hurting on and off for a few hours but I'm okay." His ego needed her to know he'd kept from complaining for a while.

He'd read stories of people whose feet had frozen, and when they took off their shoes, their toes came off in their socks. With that thought hanging over him, he untied the laces on his boots and pulled one off.

Ryan stared at his blue sock, wondering what it looked like underneath. Would the toes match the sock?

He didn't want to know and took out the now lukewarm hand warmer from his glove and placed it in his boot. When he placed it in, his foot screamed in agony.

Mina sat down next to him on the log. "No, you can't warm it up."

"I really think I should."

She yanked on his boot. "If you warm it up and it freezes again, you'll be in even worse shape."

He reached down to push her hand away, but she grabbed him and looked into his eyes. "You got to trust me on this."

He relented and pulled the warmer back out, hoping she was right.

"They'll be here soon," she said. "By night we'll be sitting in front of a fire somewhere sipping coffee, warming up from the inside out."

"Hot chocolate."

"What?"

"Coffee is so bitter unless you sweeten it. Why not go for hot chocolate?"

"Because we're adults."

"Which means we can top it with as much whipped cream as we want."

She stopped her laughter and looked pensive. "Can I have three giant marshmallows?"

"You can have a tower of marshmallows."

He scooted closer to her to share some warmth and, although she stiffened, she didn't move away. "My mom never let me have more than two. When she wasn't looking, I would sneak into the pantry and grab two more."

Ryan rotated his ankle, trying to find some position that didn't cry out to be cut off.

Mina glanced down at his feet. "I shouldn't have told you to walk. If it is frostbite, it's better to sit."

Somewhere above them and beyond their sight, the sun met the horizon. "It's the winter solstice today; I'd forgotten," Ryan said.

"Yep, I was supposed to be working all this week with people coming in for Christmas, but they canceled when I found..." She kicked the frozen ground. "When everything happened." After a moment of uneasy silence, she asked, "Why did you ask me about the body?"

They had come to a truce, one that he didn't want to violate. He didn't trust their tentative relationship enough with the entire truth, not yet. "I've done a lot of research on mountain predators. You can tell a lot about the predator by the condition of the remains."

"You seem like a sort-of intelligent person. Why are you chasing something that doesn't exist?"

"Our entire lives are spent chasing something that doesn't exist. You chase it in the hopes it will exist."

"What's that supposed to mean?"

"It could be something as simple as a paycheck or maybe as complicated as falling in love."

Mina straightened up to give him the full effect of her skepticism. "There's a difference. You have past evidence to prove future outcomes." That was the first time he could hear the pre-law in her language.

He'd learned a long time ago to pick and choose who to talk to about certain things. Even the fact he had past evidence. He'd pick another time.

They alternated pacing and sitting while the darkness crept in. Mina did a series of burpees while Ryan hopped up and down on his foot that still had feeling.

But exhaustion took over and the cold crept in.

Chapter 18

Mina awoke in a stupor of darkness. Feeling as if a house of frat boys had drunk her under the table, she pulled herself to consciousness. The blackness offered no clue of her whereabouts to her weighted brain.

Only a warm mound of clothing jogged her memory. The storm, the walk, the cabin, and Ryan. Ryan, that thought shined a flashlight through the haze.

She'd fallen asleep against Ryan, who leaned against the only solid wall in the shack. "Wake up," She shook him, but he didn't budge. Stupid, she berated herself in a panic. Sleep led to death.

She grabbed his shoulder, her fingers digging into him. "Wake up." This was now a command. She would not fail someone again. "Ryan, open your eyes."

His skin shifted under her fingers as he pulled himself out of unconsciousness. "I'm awa...," he rolled his head but couldn't lift it.

With two hands clutching his coat, she straddled his long legs stretched out in front of him. "Open your eyes." She slapped him and cried out as the pain ricocheted through her cold hand. "Wake up."

His eyes half opened. "Sorry," he mumbled.

Mina went in for a second hit but a loud rhythmic bang interrupted her. It repeated every thirty or so seconds, filling the frozen night air. Too far apart to be a woodpecker, even if one was stupid enough to be out in this weather.

Was it the rescuers trying to signal them? Sol and whoever would come would know the way to the cabin; it was a popular landmark.

She slid open the door, its rusty nailed hinge echoing across the snow. With each bang, her body tensed up. When it ceased, she tensed up more.

The incessant banging started again; this time closer.

Behind her, a disjointed voice came out of the darkness. "That's him," Ryan said, his voice a sleepwalker's lament.

She stumbled her way back to him, using her hands to guide her feet. "What does he want?" she asked, telling herself she only asked to keep him with her.

"A warning, we're in his territory." His voice came through stronger, and he stood as Mina made it to his side. "Found a partial print earlier." Ryan whistled a piercing call.

"What are you doing?"

"Calling."

She debated slapping him again, even raising her hand a few inches. A guttural scream ruptured the deceiving safety of the cabin, a sound she recognized from that day. She leaped to her feet. "It's a cougar," she whispered.

Where were the rescuers?

Ryan fumbled around in the darkness while Mina tried to convince herself everything was normal. "I found a stick," he whispered.

Banging her shins against who knows what, she made her way to the rickety door that couldn't keep back the Mormons, let alone a prowling cougar.

Last fall a cougar had attacked a lone biker, dragging his body back to its den. That had been a recovery no one forgot.

She pressed against the door while kicking around with her feet for anything she could use to blockade the door. While cougars, or whatever that was, would usually back down from an aggressive human, the beast would have the advantage in the dark.

Ryan came up beside her, "Try this." The "stick" he'd found was a small log about five inches in diameter. She wedged it up under what remained of a door handle while he attempted to push it into the frozen ground.

The incessant banging returned.

"If it's Bigfoot, he's not usually an aggressor," Ryan said in a whisper. "This is more of a warning that we're in his territory, and he's the dominant."

The urge to slap him returned in force. She took a step back and if she'd had enough light, she would've glared him to submission. "Aaaahhh," she screamed at the top of her lungs.

"What are you doing?"

"Asserting my dominance. Whatever is out there, and it's not Bigfoot, already knows we're here."

Ryan grasped her sleeve. "You saw what happened to that missing skier. You don't think he tried to yell?"

She pulled her arm out of his grasp. "You don't know," she said, giving up on any pretense of whispering.

"I know what killed him. I know it because I found a body like the one you did. Only I was too young or too stupid to run for help. I stood there, peeing myself, as the creature hunched over part of the body."

They pressed against the door, waiting for whatever stalked them.

Chapter 19

The rescuers came not long after dawn.

They explained they'd attempted to come the night before but almost lost a snowmobile and its driver into a ravine hidden by a layer of snow. They needed time and light.

Mina credited the noise in the woods, which was not Bigfoot, with saving them. Had it not woken her and scared the bejeebers out of them, they would've slumbered their way to death.

Phil and James had been rescued the day before by a Snowcat brought up from the bottom of the canyon. James had to be life-flighted to the nearest hospital. Sol said he was unconscious when they found him but breathing. Phil was cold but otherwise unscathed.

It almost cost two lives to save one. Mina didn't like that math.

She sat at the clinic in a waiting room that doubled as an office. Ryan had been taken back first on account of his feet and there being only one nurse and doctor.

Sol sat next to her, alternating standing and sitting. Neutral and sitting was the only gear she could manage. Someone had handed her an egg sandwich from Beth's, a café that opened each day at 4 am, filled with greasy goodness.

"Sol," she said after eating too much too fast that made her a bit queasy and forced a pause, "did I make the right call?"

"I don't know."

She'd messed up; she knew that and regretted asking his confirmation. The eggs caught in the back of her throat, and she forced them down. "We should've stayed in the car."

"I don't know." Why had she picked this maddening man to be her mentor? "Nor do you, nor will you ever. Part of our job means making decisions under difficult circumstances, which you did. You'll waste time second-guessing."

She pulled off another layer she wore as her body realized they sat indoors. "So what, I just assume every decision I make is the right one?"

"When you make a mistake, you own it. But an imperfect outcome doesn't necessarily mean you messed up. And when you weigh life, you accept that someone may be hurt by a decision you make."

She shot to her feet, but dizziness from hypothermia and hunger sat her right back down again. She stood again, more slowly. "I'm going to go see how things are going with Ryan." She needed to know she didn't screw up and didn't want a philosophy lesson.

Down a small hallway, the voices of Ryan and the doctor echoed back. "Mind if I check in?" she called out.

"You got a bullet I can bite?" Ryan said with grit in his voice.

She turned a corner and had to swallow a gasp at what had been in Ryan's boots. His toes looked purple, like someone dropped an anvil on them.

He had them dipped into a tray of water. Ryan clenched the handles of the chair he sat in; his eyes squeezed shut. Mina wanted to apologize but that would be more about her than him. "What do you need?" She forced a light tone, uncomfortable to admit the seriousness of it all.

She tried to heed Sol's warning against second-guessing. Four people came out alive, she reminded herself.

"A knife to cut these toes off. Having them gone can't be worse than this," he said through clenched teeth.

She leveled a stare at the doctor, Peter, who also moonlighted at the resort in first aid. He stood behind Ryan, hanging an IV. "Hopefully it'll kick in soon."

"You don't have anything better than water to warm him up?"

"We have to warm him up slowly if we want to save the toes."

Ryan didn't react to this. That conversation must've already happened.

"Ryan," Peter said. "I'm going to check out Mina while the drugs kick in before we get to the next part.

He managed a nod. "Don't tell me what the next part is."

Mina tried to protest. "I'm fine; stay with him."

"Seen yourself in a mirror?" Peter asked.

"Not if I can help it."

"Follow me."

Peter took her behind another curtain where he soaked a Q-tip in disinfectant. "You've got a few patches of frostbite on your cheeks and nose that's already blistering. By tomorrow, it'll look like you had a major sunburn. I'm afraid you won't win any beauty pageants for a while."

She managed a shaky smile through the burning sensation as he applied the disinfectant to her face, a small glimpse of what Ryan must be going through. "What? My face is my moneymaker."

"Speaking of which. You can't be outside for very long for the next few weeks. And when you are, and I'm talking walking to your house from your car, your face needs to be covered."

"Peter," she said without a hint of a smile, "being outside *is* my moneymaker. I can't lose that income."

"I know, but if you want to heal without your face sloughing off and scarring then you'll listen. Choice is yours."

Sol called out. "How's it coming?"

"Apparently, I'm on my way to being Scarface," Mina said, casting a dirty look at Peter.

"You'll heal." Sol came into the room as the doctor left it. "I got word from the hospital in Summit; James is conscious. He's responding well to oxygen and drugs."

She sank back onto the plastic examination chair. She would never forgive herself if what she put Ryan through had been for nothing. "I know his kids. Couldn't imagine having to tell them I let their dad die. I don't know if Ryan will find it a fair trade though."

"You have to learn to live with this decision. Otherwise, you won't be able to make the next one."

She stared down at her bare feet, where she'd stuck on an adhesive foot warmer she'd stolen from behind the nursing desk. "Where's my Jeep?"

"It'll be a few days until they can dig it out. Let me know when you're ready, and I'll drive you home."

"I need to go see Ryan; he's in a lot of hurt." She stood and a wave of dizziness forced her back down. Sol reached out a steadying arm, but she waved him off.

Ryan's voice carried from around the corner. "I don't mind losing the pinky toe; it's always been a crooked, weird-looking thing." His drugs must be kicking in.

Peter's voice boomed back. "I'll chop it off now then."

"You'll need a bullet to bite on," Mina called out as she stood, this time more slowly.

The irreverent doctor pushed back the curtain to allow her in. She flinched at the sight of Ryan's toes fully out of the water. Around the edges of the blue, the skin looked white and waxy, blistering into nasty round bumps. "That's no good."

Ryan shrugged, not meeting her eyes. She could read the anxiety behind his joking. "Doctor said there's a chance he might be able to save them."

Peter put a note into the iPad he carried. "There's a treatment I've been using with some success. It uses a laser to get oxygen to the infected areas and helps save the skin, if it isn't dead yet. I'm going to get you both some sample pain medication to get you by for the next few days." He left them alone.

Mina stood next to Ryan shifting from foot to foot, unsure of what to say or do. "Sorry about your toes."

"The tissue isn't dead yet." His face dropped and he took a breath. "But that's not what's worrying me the most."

She dropped to the chair the doctor had abandoned. "What's wrong?"

"What are you going to look like when your nose falls off?"

She stared at him speechless until a small smile broke through his moroseness. "You jerk." She cocked her head at him with a smirk. "Lucky for you, I'll be too busy running circles around your shortened feet to care."

He stared back at his toes as if analyzing them. "I had the biggest feet in sixth grade and that included the ninth-grade kids. I guess I could stand to lose a few inches."

"You'd have to buy new shoes and that gets pricey." Mina took a turn to study her own feet, wrapped in purple hospital socks with rubber on the soles. "I'm sorry," she whispered.

"Nothing to be sorry for," he said without a hint of frustration. "It was necessary."

Peter pushed back the curtain. "Sorry, you two. It's last call, and I'm the designated driver."

Mina stood while Ryan fumbled for a pair of crutches sitting next to him. "You don't have to take me home. Sol said he would," she said to Peter.

"I'm not. Stretch here should really spend one more night in a hospital, but we're not set up for that and the storm isn't letting anybody out of this valley for a few days. He's coming home with me tonight."

Mina helped Ryan to Peter's car. "I'll call you tomorrow," she said as she shut the door on him, careful not to nick his toes.

Chapter 20

Mina drugged herself into an early slumber and woke up with a gray dawn struggling through her window.

Several text messages filled her phone, including three from her mom. It took years of conditioning to convince her mother if she didn't respond to a text right away it wasn't because she was dead, only out of service. Apparently, word had gotten to her mom about Mina's night in the canyon. She made a quick call that turned into a long call.

"Mina, why did a sheriff of the law tell me you were missing?"

"Mom, it's okay. I got snowed in and couldn't get phone service. You wouldn't believe the amounts we got. The skiing is going to be once-in-a-lifetime. You should come out." Once upon a time, her mom had learned to ski beside Mina. That was before her father's lay-off and Mina's student loans had wiped out their retirement.

"Are you safe?" The last word came out with a half-sob.

She liked to roll her eyes at her mother's constant worry but at least Mina was loved. She didn't come home for one night and people noticed, unlike their John.

Part of the reason she lived at such a distance from her parents was that same love she had for them. The guilt at close proximity was too much. They'd lived and breathed the American dream, and it spat them out. They'd worked hard for Mina to go to the best schools, get a law degree, and support them in their retirement.

Her parents still worked full-time and then some. She'd moved all the student loans to her name, but the damage had been done. She could run away from expectations but never responsibility.

"I'm safe; I promise."

"Will you be safe tomorrow and the next day?"

"Will you?"

"Yes." Her mother would never be deflected. "Tell me why a sheriff called me to tell me my daughter did not show up for work?"

Mina thought up five lies, none of which her mother would believe. "I'm working part-time for the sheriff's office. No biggie, I pick up trash and direct traffic."

Her mom's sigh vibrated through the phone. "I wish you would settle. You are so smart, but you don't always act smart."

"I've got to go."

As she hung up, she stared at her phone. Her mom was right; she didn't always act smart.

From the moment she met Ryan, she'd known something felt off about him.

It took a couple of different search terms to find an article about a body found in pieces in the Shasta Lake area of Northern California.

Partial remains were discovered in the mountains above Sunshine Camp, a summer camp for teenagers. According to Sheriff Broden, it appeared the body had only been there a few days, and they are still determining the identification.

Sources from the camp say the body had been found in pieces. "There was a whole leg 20 feet out," said an employee of the camp who wished to remain anonymous.

The remains were first found by a fourteen-year-old boy who had become lost on a group hike. The juvenile spent the night in the woods before finding his way out in the morning light to call for help.

Mina didn't last ten minutes in the forest after finding the body yet Ryan, still a child, spent the night in the woods. The paper had published another article a few days later.

Remains found Tuesday at Sunshine Camp have been identified as Hannah Eliason, a camp counselor who worked at the camp for several seasons.

Sheriff Broden said, while they're conducting a full investigation, it's most likely an animal attack. "I advise people recreating in the area to carry bear spray, keep all pets on a leash, and above all, don't go into the woods alone."

There weren't any other articles she could find beyond an obituary, which didn't mention the cause of death. It did, however, mention Meg's love of the outdoors and children.

She called the California office, but the sheriff had long since retired. Once she claimed to be from the company managing his pension and had a concern about a large amount being withdrawn, they quickly gave her his cell phone. He didn't answer but she left a message, this time with the truth.

As she hung up, Mina's phone buzzed. An unknown number called her, and she picked up. "Hello."

"Mina, it's Ryan. How are you?"

Not wanting him to know she'd spent the last hour digging into his life, she faked a lighter tone. "Cold, how are you?"

"Warmer than I was yesterday at this same time."

"How are your feet?"

"Same, but I have to ignore the urge to stuff them in a vat of boiling water. Peter says not to expose them to extreme heat and, apparently, that qualifies as extreme."

She wanted to ask him about the body but surprised herself with the words, "What are you doing on Christmas Eve?"

"Why?"

Why, indeed? "I don't know; I just thought maybe you'd want to meet up for lunch. You probably have plans so don't—"

"I'd like that."

"Okay, then." She hung up before she could blurt out any other dumb ideas.

Sol was her next call. "You bored yet?" He said by way of hello.

She'd been home for all of a half-day. "Yes, very."

"Thought you might appreciate an update. The wayward Charlie surfaced."

Mina didn't know to be relieved their dead man wasn't a local or frustrated they still didn't know who their victim was. She chose both emotions. "Where was the idiot?"

"Drunk enough he's not fully sure, but sober enough he surfaced for work.

And I called that ski instructor you mentioned. Her missing date texted her back the day after you two talked. He apologized but said he wanted to get to the airport before the storm."

"So, we've got nothing?"

"That about sums it up. But I don't want him to fall through the cracks. With the holiday coming up, we're boosting patrols. Clint and I will be running ragged. I know you don't have much experience but if you want to look through the reports and…"

"Yes. I'm in."

Chapter 21

Ryan checked his email, starting with the newest first. Lucky for him, the last email telling him he was fired saved a whole lot of time reading the previous fifty.

He could probably reply and explain himself, maybe get his job back. With his fingers hovering over the keyboard, he reconsidered. With a decent savings and some stock options, Ryan could take a few months. His skills were such there'd be another job sooner or later.

Maybe Mina had rubbed off on him in the mountains. Maybe he was finally ready to examine his skeletons. Either way, he closed his laptop and called Phil for a ride to the store. He would need better gear to go up next time.

As Ryan crawled into Phil's car—his Range Rover had yet to be towed out of the canyon—spasms of pain shot up his leg, which he did his best to ignore.

His best wasn't good enough and Phil watched him, guilt lining his face. "I'm sorry I let you walk out."

Ryan shrugged; his shoulders were the one part of his body not sore. "We all survived. How bad did it get with James?"

"He was fairly out of it. For a while there I didn't think he was going to wake up."

"Good thing he had you there."

"He could've had better company." Phil glanced out the window and looked as if he wanted to say something.

"Want to grab lunch?" Ryan asked.

"No, I can't. I got a phone call with my lawyer about some stuff."

Sometimes Ryan forgot about his friend's previous identity as a tech tycoon. Phil could probably get Ryan another job in a week, but he liked having a friendship that existed outside the real world.

They pulled into the local sporting goods store where Ryan intended to buy anything and everything that could keep him warm. A salesperson was showing him battery-operated boot heaters, which he would most definitely be buying, when he spotted James across the store.

James didn't seem to recognize them, which made sense. It'd been dark, and he'd been in a sorry state when they'd all met. A woman stood next to him, probably his wife. She glanced over and nudged her husband before whispering in his ear.

The man broke into a wide smile and quickly came over. "Man, I can't thank you and Mina enough. Doing what you did saved my life."

Ryan unconsciously rubbed the leg of his bad foot. "It was more her. She was determined to go, and I didn't want to stay in the car with your sorry state."

James laughed. "You made the right call." Thanks had been offered and the receiving man acted like it was no big deal. Man Code upheld.

James took Phil's hand and shook it. "Sorry, I didn't recognize you at first. That day or so is a blur."

Phil looked down at the ground and mumbled something, maybe a 'you're welcome' before walking off.

"Is he doing all right?" Cate asked. "The few times I've met him he seemed a lot more talkative."

"You know him?" Ryan shouldn't be surprised. Phil could land on the moon and find someone he'd been acquainted with.

"Only a little. We met at the lodge and talked mostly about our kids and Christmas. I take it, you are a Bigfoot hunter like him?"

Ryan flinched in surprise. "How did you know?"

"It's a small town. All you have to do is listen and you learn everyone's secrets, eventually."

"What are you out and about doing?" Ryan asked, wanting to change the subject

"Getting outfitted for the winter," James said. "My last job was in Dubai. I don't think I'll be warm until August." He rubbed the scruff on his face. "I'm trying to grow a beard, but that might be a lost cause." His white hair matched the color of his skin. Dubai's desert sun hadn't found him out of the office.

Ryan hadn't shaved in a week and his own beard had thickened up. "No kidding. This cold is unbelievable."

Cate reached up and kissed her husband on the cheek. "Not too thick. I'm going to track down Phil. I want to talk to him about organizing an event for these Bigfoot hunters. Try to drum up some business in the off-season."

"Ryan," James said. "Remind me where you're from."

Before Ryan could respond, he caught sight of a man whom Ryan did not want to catch sight of him. "Sorry, I've got to run." He backed down the aisle and rounded the corner with his eye on the door when Lane Jenkins stepped in front of him.

Lane clapped him on the shoulder as if they were old friends. "Ryan, I knew you would be here."

Ryan regretted a lot of things in life and trusting this man with his story was high on that list. "Yep, needed some gear."

Lane laughed as if they were on a first date. "I mean in Lost Gorge. It must feel good to be close to vindication. Even a lot of Squatchers think you made your story up. Bunch of bleeding hearts who think Squatch is a gentle giant. I'd love to get your perspective on my documentary."

"I'm not going on camera."

"I wouldn't think of it." Lane followed Ryan outside. "Look, I found a guy in town who can get me into an area known for its sightings. You have to cross through private property to get to it so there's no going up without him. I want you with me."

Ryan stopped to face him. "Why? I'm not changing my mind. And let's be honest, you really don't believe in Bigfoot; you're only here to capitalize on a dead man."

"I'm agnostic, which makes me open. But it doesn't matter what I believe;

what matters is you do. This area is legit, and it's less than a mile from the attack. You want to find anything, it's a good place to start."

Ryan wasn't above using this guy to get closer to the truth. "When do we leave?"

Chapter 22

Mina took Sol up on his offer. Despite it being two days before Christmas and the start of her busiest stretch, the resort had yet to rebound from the gruesome discovery.

Her clients had canceled for the week, making reservations elsewhere. The snow would've drawn people back had it come soon enough they hadn't already swapped one set of plans for another. At least this season she had another option. She pushed open the sheriff's office door to see Sol hovering over Clint's computer.

"Where's Clint?" she asked.

Sol looked up, disapproval carving his face. "You shouldn't be outside. I thought you'd work from home."

"I'm not; I'm in."

One of these days she hoped to force an unintended laugh from her boss. It appeared today would not be that day. "Clint took the day off. His wife wasn't feeling too well, and they didn't have anyone to take care of their son. Why are you out?"

"I'm officially full-time," she said, surprising herself.

Sol walked her through what had been done in the investigation in the last few days. And while much had been done, not much had been accomplished. Still no identity and no official cause of death.

"The shuttle driver remembers a single man riding up the morning of from town. He noticed the skier because he seemed to be a tourist but most tourists travel in groups."

"Where did he pick him up?" Mina asked.

"He's not sure, but we've hit all the hotels and contacted everyone registered over the weekend. No one is unaccounted for. Look through the files with fresh eyes. Maybe you'll see something."

He left her at the office while he went out to patrol the highway. On holidays people had the tendency to take a break from adhering to the laws, and he would serve to remind them.

Before she dug too deep, the door opened, bringing in a rush of arctic air. Mina unconsciously pulled her scarf up around her face. Cate blasted through the door with the cold, her cheeks red and her eyes bright.

"Hey, Cate," Mina said, perking up. She wasn't much used to the solitude and quiet.

"Hi, how are you?" She shed her coat. "The kids don't want to ski with any other instructor. I took them up yesterday to do a few runs and all they did was tell me what Coach Mina said about everything."

"I'm impressed you went with them. You're learning fast."

"Not as fast as them." She glanced around the office. "Sol around?"

"No, he went out on patrol."

"Shoot, I wanted to ask him about organizing an event. Thought maybe we could capitalize on the Bigfoot thing and do a gathering here."

"A gathering?"

"Yeah, I've been talking to some of these guys. They host gatherings with events and things. Might help us draw in a crowd for January between holiday weekends."

Mina did not want more crazy people climbing through the mountains hunting shadows. "I don't know; what's the city say?"

"Do whatever you can to increase tourists if you want to keep your job," said Cate without a hint of irony.

Mina didn't have a good response to that. "Sorry."

"Don't worry." She winked. "As my husband says, I tend to exaggerate."

"How is James?" Mina asked to change the subject.

"I think that man dropped two grand on winter clothes yesterday. Not sure if he's warmed up from being stuck."

"He'll need those if he stays all winter."

"That's a big if."

Mina's phone rang with the number she'd called the California sheriff with. "I've got to answer this."

"No problem. Tell Sol to call me."

Mina picked up the phone to talk to the former sheriff, who very well remembered a body from twenty years ago.

"Some things you don't forget." Pain and shock still filled the sheriff's voice as he described the body. "It was just in pieces. We get animal attacks often enough but that was something at a whole other level."

"What do you mean?" Mina figured she knew the answer but didn't want to fill in his words.

"Decimated, I guess. The poor girl hadn't been missing that long, but we never found all of her. I figured bear, but there weren't slashes on the carcass, only pieces. Same with her clothes, torn apart but not shredded like you'd expect."

"What did you decide happened?"

He scoffed on the other end of the line. "You don't get to decide what happened."

"What did Ryan say? I mean the kid who found her."

A heavy moment of silence filled the phone. "Who are you really?"

Mina had no choice to explain their situation and Ryan showing up in it. There was no reason not to, but she felt a tinge of guilt like she was somehow betraying Ryan.

"That kid is still telling everyone it's Bigfoot, huh."

"Is that what he said back then?"

"Not in so many words."

"Do you think he had something to do with it?" she asked, trying to hide the anxiety in her voice.

"I don't know." He paused. "He was just a scrawny kid. Tall enough but all bones. You know he found the body close to dusk but didn't get out to find help until morning. Can't imagine what that night would've been like for him."

Mina could, and she'd only lasted fifteen minutes before fleeing for help.

"I did wonder with his background if there wasn't more to it," the sheriff said.

"His background?"

"Yeah, the camp was a place for juvenile delinquents to get straightened out."

Ryan had lied; told her his parents had sent him to camp to get him away from video games.

"He didn't have a record." He continued. "But all the boys who went there had to have a reason. And I did think there was something the kid held back, something he wouldn't say. Whether that was intentional or the fear pushed it down, I don't know."

"Can you think of anything to help us, anything at all?"

"Keep it as quiet as you can. You wouldn't believe the madness that descended here. Between those people chasing Bigfoot, the hunters going for bear, and everybody else in a panic; we had to rescue no less than five people lost in the wilderness. The body count could've easily grown."

Advice that was a little too late. "Thanks, I'll call you if I need something else."

A text message flashed. She sighed when she saw it was from Ryan.

We still on for lunch tomorrow? I can meet you at the resort.

Her finger hovered over the keys as a typing bubble appeared.

I figured you'd be skiing.

She typed out a response.

Doctor said we should be inside.

Of course. How about we eat inside and call it a compromise?

Okay, but I want hot chocolate.

He replied with a winky face emoji.

Mina shouldn't meet him. He blamed Bigfoot for crying out loud. He honestly, truly thought a mythical animal ripped a human being apart. He was a distraction, and she didn't have time for a distraction—not in winter and especially not this winter.

Still, he left the safety of the Jeep to walk out with her. He didn't have to do that.

Chapter 23

On Christmas Eve morning, the skies cleared and the temperatures plummeted. Had Mina been anyone else, she would've huddled inside by a fire wrapping gifts.

Her friends had been blowing up her phone with texts the last few days. The best powder in a decade, they said. Epic couldn't begin to describe it.

Ski patrol, including Patrick, had been going nonstop performing avalanche control. Their opening up of new terrain would be the perfect Christmas present to every powder hound.

Ignoring the frostbite and doctor's orders, Mina found herself at the edge of a bowl with no tracks. The closed canyon and beast rumors had kept out the tourists and only those lucky enough to be locals could lay claim to this winter wonder.

Patrick waited behind her with a GoPro on his helmet and avalanche beacons on both their backs. A handwritten sign had graced the ticket window that morning:

To get on Summit chairlift, guests must have the following:
  A shovel
  A beacon
  A buddy

Everybody had to take a selfie in front of it and post it on Instagram. The resort couldn't pay for better advertisement than that. Monster or no, the road up the canyon would fill in the next few weeks.

With a shallow breath through the small holes of her face mask, Mina shoved off the edge of the bowl and dropped into the powder. She immediately sank to her hips and knew there would be very little turning today. The snow demanded long, fast skiing and she gladly acquiesced.

Patrick dropped in behind her as did a few others. The hoots and hollers of adults who knew how to have fun like kids echoed across the mountain.

They rode the lift back up basking in the glow of just being them. "This is it for me," Patrick said. "I've got to go place some fences before the resort gets more crowded."

Her face rubbed against the mask, the sting reminding her of the toll each run took. "I should call it, too. Plus, I'm meeting someone for lunch."

"Is it that guy?" The last word came out dripped in unsaid insults.

"What guy is that?"

"The guy you got lost in the woods with?"

"Yes."

"He's lucky you were there to save his butt," Patrick muttered. "Skinny nothing."

"When did you meet him?

"Saw him at the store with all those wackos. You can do better."

"I suppose." She wanted her tone to convey his jealousy didn't matter to her. Whether it did or it didn't would be a question she would continually push down the road.

They split up at the top, and she headed to a place she'd been avoiding—the grove where she'd found the body. She slipped through an opening in the rope, a gate marked as experts only, and dropped into the trees.

The bright day belittled the bloody event that had taken place.

Mina didn't expect to find anything like tracks; the series of storms would've taken care of that. She wasn't sure if she expected to find anything, or if she needed to face what had been haunting her.

The few strips of crime scene tape she'd hung about four feet off the snow level now lay wrapped in the snow. She pulled out what she could and stuck the pieces in her pocket to dispose of later. Hers weren't the only tracks in the area as other skiers had ripped through the powder.

Why did the victim climb up here? There were only two ways into this area: one would require skiing in but that would mean getting off at the top and dropping in. The other would mean a climb up a five or so-foot cliff that had laid bare that day, wearing ski boots in a blizzard.

In a storm, instinct would've encouraged him downhill or at least through easier terrain. A good reason why everyone insisted it had to be an animal attack. Something killed him below and then dragged his body up here.

Where had he actually died? And where was he when she first climbed through these trees? Had his body already been moved?

If so, the blood in the trees hadn't been there when she first passed through. Maybe something killed him below without leaving much blood. Then something dragged his body up into the trees where it had been torn apart. If not by an animal, then what?

Mina, her legs spent from holding a line in the powder, pushed into the trees. She turned around a few tree wells, careful to stay out of their vortexes, and slid to a stop. The pines were tight here and didn't allow for speed.

Not far from where she stood had been the worst of the body. Like before, the sun didn't shine through the thick branches and no sounds of other skiers or the chairlift broke through the silence.

She whistled and then shook her head at her own stupidity. Then cursed herself even more as she couldn't help but listen back. She'd spent far too much time with Ryan.

The cliff she'd skied off the first time had disappeared under a sharp bank of snow. It only took a few minutes to be back under the lift.

This spot would be the closest he could've fallen to where they found him. If he'd fallen.

If? He got on the lift, and he never got off. What other answer could there be? If he did fall, that was horribly bad luck. Fall off a chairlift, get injured, and be attacked by wild animals. All in a fairly short time frame. She'd skied the entire run within a half-hour of him being reported missing. He wasn't there.

If he didn't fall, what then?

He jumped off and then somehow still died? He was pushed? By whom?

99

He'd loaded the lift alone.

Mina skied down the mountain and headed to the chairlift. Her luck held. Tim ran it and no one waited in line. The better powder was on the other side of the resort in the chutes and bowls that had been opened only that morning.

Tim nodded as she shuffled up. "Don't tell me how amazing the powder is."

"Why? Aren't you going up on your lunch break?"

"Nope," he scowled. "Everyone called in sick today." He used his fingers to put quote marks around "sick." "Don't nobody tell you it pays to be the boss's son." Tim's dad had been general manager for fifteen years or so.

"Not enough skiers on the mountain to ski this out before tomorrow. You'll get yours."

"Better."

"Can I ask you something?"

"Sure."

"Do you think about that day, ever?"

Tim didn't take his eyes off the chairs as each one went by. "Every day."

"I do, too. Wonder how I didn't see him when I came down."

"I wonder if I had just closed up a few minutes earlier. I wanted to, you know. The resort had emptied out. Before him, I had one skier that entire hour." The radio crackled next to him. He paused but it was for another lift. "I was pulling the ropes off the lift line when he pulled up, and I just waved him through. Didn't mention the conditions, nothing."

Mina had been so focused on her own guilt, it didn't occur to her the guilt went around. "It was up to the resort to close the lift, not you." A skier came through and they paused until she was on her way up. "Did you see what he looked like?" Mina continued.

"Like any other skier. Dark clothes and a helmet with his goggles down. I told Sol he didn't say a word; only nodded." Tim left the chair to fix one of the ropes marking the lift line that had tipped over. "I was taking down the ropes, and he didn't need help. You getting on?"

She hadn't been on that chairlift since that day. Even earlier she had

100

dropped into the trees from another nearby peak. "Yeah, might as well." She shuffled forward and the chair lifted her off the ground.

This chair mainly crossed over open runs until it neared the top where it went over a ridgeline, maybe only fifteen feet from the ground and between two trees. One tree was close enough to touch and over the years people had thrown Mardi Gras beads and, in some cases, their underwear into the pine. The spot where the body was found was maybe 50 yards away.

He could've jumped off here. People certainly had before in attempts to curry likes on Instagram. Riders leap off to the cheers of their photographing buddies below yelling, "Send it."

Most of the time the resort didn't know it had happened until the tagged videos showed up on social media or ski patrol got called in to haul off the failed sends.

That day, though, would've been idiotic to attempt a jump. There hadn't been enough snow to cushion the fall and with the warmer temps and then cold wind, the snow had iced over.

Mina couldn't get over that thought, *if* he'd fallen.

By the time she got to the top it was noon. Ryan would be waiting for her—another mystery to solve. She zoomed down the run, unable to enjoy the bumps and powder any longer.

Mina stopped in the bathroom before meeting Ryan. Her hair a smashed, black mess of tangles she hadn't taken the time to braid in the morning couldn't be helped.

Behind her a toilet flushed and Adrienne walked out wearing a uniform, proving someone still worked. As if reading her mind, she smiled and said, "Kids of locals, who didn't want to miss the powder." She put on her jacket. "They were all picked up just now; no full dayers and no tips."

"Sounds about right."

"So, what's up with you and Patrick? I heard he moved back in with Wes. Weren't you two living together?"

"No." She didn't like to talk about her love life or lack thereof to someone whose name she barely knew, but she would not let that rumor fly. "I don't know where he was shacked up." *Or who with,* she added under her breath.

"So, if you're not going out with him…" Adrienne left the question unsaid but understood. They were an incestuous bunch in this small world, which required not caring or pretending not to care as couples disintegrated and reformed.

"The pickings are slim this season, aren't they?" Mina was allowed a small dig, wasn't she? "I heard that guy who stood you up called back."

Still, as slim as the pickings were, men outnumbered women, making the odds on the female's side. Mina tried to run her fingers through her hair to comb out the semblance of a braid.

"Yeah. Apparently, he's on his way to Africa and said he'd be out of phone service for a few months. The life of a reporter. Surprised he even thought to text me. See you later, I'm meeting someone." Adrienne dashed out the door.

Mina's phone buzzed. Ryan had arrived in the parking lot. She beat him to the dining room, where few people sat. Some skiers, like Patrick, would swallow a sandwich on the chairlift and call it good. Others would trail in a little later, holding out until the powder had turned their legs into mush.

Speaking of mushy legs, Ryan came through the door, walking with a limp—if you could have a limp on both feet. Going by the redness of his face and his stride, he did not spend the morning taking it easy.

Mina shook her head at him as he sat down. In response to her unspoken chastisement, he broke into a boyish grin and returned the gesture. She was in no place to judge. They ordered hot chocolates to get started.

"Did you find Bigfoot?" Mina asked after the waiter left. "Can I make an arrest?"

He took off the first of several layers. "Not today." It was his turn to tsk at her. "I thought you were going to keep your face covered up."

"I did."

"You look like you're growing a new layer of skin."

"Don't those rich ladies get chemical peels or such things? This is my version. How are the dead toes you've been walking on?"

"Coming back to life in a very painful way. I didn't walk too far."

"I didn't ski too much."

The waiter brought their hot chocolates. "Can you bring some marshmallows for my friend?" Ryan asked.

"No, I'm good." Mina protested.

Ryan ignored her. "Please bring what you would consider an embarrassing amount of marshmallows," he told the waiter.

The waiter nodded. "The toddler amount." He walked off.

"Ryan."

"You said in the cabin that's what you wanted."

"Now I look silly."

"Mina, I can't imagine you ever looking silly." He took a sip of his, leaving a large whip cream mustache. "Embrace being odd."

"You would know."

Their burgers came, and they dug in without speaking. The cold worked up an appetite that demanded satiation. She didn't know how the others did it with a quick sandwich on the lift. "How was the skiing?" he asked once half his burger and steak fries were gone.

A smile cracked her face and a blister. She flinched. "Totally worth it. How was your search today?"

"Totally worth it. You know there are people who go their entire lives without something to get crazy passionate about."

She thought of her parents who seemed to lose joy as the years went on. She tried to convince them to take a class, join a club—anything but Netflix. "They're comfortable, I guess."

A familiar voice interrupted their conversation. "Mina, Ryan." James stood at their table with Cate and the kids behind him. The kids rushed around to hug Mina and launched into an itinerary of their morning, which included skiing their mother through trees.

Cate bopped the closest twin with an affectionate fist on her helmet. "Dragged me is more like it."

"You and I will have to go without the kids," Mina said. "Get you up to speed."

"It's okay," one of the twins said. "Mom skied with us to this little cabin in the woods."

"Oh, yeah," Mina said. "Snowshoe Sam's cabin. The oldest building at the resort. Lots of fun trails in there for kids." Those runs weren't too far from where the body was found. It was good to see people making their way over. Maybe the snow would bring back the crowds.

James reached out to shake Ryan's hand and nodded at Mina. "I was just telling Cate we need to invite you two over for dinner. Thank you properly."

Mina resisted the urge to reach up and scratch her raw nose. "You would've done the same for us."

He put an arm around Cate, pulling her close. "You got me home to my family for Christmas." With his other arm, he grabbed his daughter who'd drifted off a few steps.

"Ryan," Cate said. "I've been trying to get a hold of Phil about organizing a Bigfoot gathering, but he's proving as allusive as the beast. What do you think? We could do it during the slow season but announce it now while we have—"

"Cate," James said. "We're all standing in our ski boots; let's get off our feet. You guys can talk later."

"Of course." James hustled them away as she said over her shoulder. "I'll call."

They finished their meals and while Ryan offered to pay, he didn't argue when she refused.

"Can I get a ride back to town?" he asked. "Phil dropped me off. I'm back staying with him."

Mina glanced out the window to the blinding sunlight, though the temps still hovered in the single digits.

"You're not going back out there, are you?" Ryan asked.

She gave off an exaggerated sigh. "No, much as I'm not worried about scarring, I don't want the nose to fall off completely. Stupid frostbite." A flash of guilt filled her as she watched him struggle to his feet. She didn't risk losing a toe. Kind of needed toes for skiing, surfing, and a whole lot of other stuff.

They climbed into the Jeep and the questions she'd been needing to ask couldn't wait anymore, like holding on to a bladder when you finally reach a toilet.

"What did you see, Ryan?"

"Something I'm sorry you had to experience." He slammed the door shut but kept his face calm. "I don't like to remember it."

"I ran a check on you, and I talked to the sheriff in California."

"Bet he had a good story for you."

"He thought you thought you were telling the truth, mostly." She cranked up the heater. "But he also thought you weren't being honest about something. And he wondered about your background, what with the camp being for juvies."

Ryan leaned his forehead against the side window. "I wasn't a juvenile delinquent. The camp worked with the state, but it also took in other kids. My parents didn't do that great of job checking it out. They just wanted me out of their hair for the summer."

Mina could whine about her parents with the best of them, but they were at every teacher night, band performance, and school play. They were the ones who snapped her into a pair of skis at age three.

"What happened out there, Ryan?"

"The body was a girl, a counselor at the camp," Ryan said, his voice fading like a memory.

Chapter 24

Fourteen-year-old Ryan had tried to catch up with the others, but his gym shoe slipped on a moss-covered rock. He'd had only recently obtained his height and hadn't yet learned how to control it. He hit the ground hard. Gasping for breath only brought pain, and he curled up in the mud until the burning in his side stopped.

"Don't cry," he said aloud, in case the others returned but he really, really wanted to. When he lifted his t-shirt, his young mind was sure to find a bone sticking out of his stomach. No protruding bone, though it felt like one ought to.

He cussed his parents in his head. Despite a few hundred miles between them, that wasn't something he dared to do out loud.

Three choices faced Ryan: hike up, hike down, or stay put.

Hiking up was out of the question. The planned hike went in a giant circle, and he'd never catch up. Waiting was worthless—only one counselor accompanied the twenty or so boys. The counselor was in front. He only stopped to mock and wouldn't notice one random boy missing.

Ryan knew he had only one choice—hike back out.

Each step brought a considerable groan. He tried to figure out a way to breathe only out of his right lung but couldn't master that.

The fog descended with a light mist, and Ryan didn't have a coat. He hadn't felt cold since he turned twelve and his feet shot out the bottom of his pants. His mother said she could feel heat blowing off him like smoke off a fire. His stomach rumbled, but it always did.

With the fog, he lost all sense of distance—not that he ever had a good sense of it before. As long as he stuck to the trail, he'd be fine. At least that's what he told himself when a few teardrops made it past his defenses.

"I'm eating two hamburgers for dinner," he said. "Don't care what they say. Maybe even three." He kicked a rock more embedded into the mud than he anticipated. The pain in his toe went straight to his ribs. He swore with a boy's delight that no one could tell him to stop.

The half-hour it should've taken him to make it to the lodge stretched into an hour. Between the gray fog and dark green trees, the landscape blurred into a bad watercolor painting.

Ryan shivered as the fog turned into a heavier spray. The trail stopped short of a waterfall; its source hidden in the rocks above.

"Wish we'd stopped here on the way up. Wait, why didn't we?" Come to think of it, he didn't recall them passing it by, and he would've remembered. "I stayed on the trail," he yelled to the empty woods. Nothing, not even a bird answered back.

"Maybe I went up instead of down," he said to the dark green forest so thick with leaves and moss, he could barely see a tree trunk. "Must've gone up."

He followed his muddy footprints back up the trail. The least he could do was return to where he'd fallen.

With each step, the pain grew, clamping on his body to punish him for daring to walk. Darkness crept on; he'd missed dinner.

The whistle. He smacked his head at his stupidity. That morning he'd won a whistle in a potato sack competition. The little orange piece of plastic wasn't much but when he put it to his lips, a small sound did come out. He blew harder. The thick pines muffled the screeching whistle; someone would have to be super close to hear him.

He sank against a giant boulder, leaning against it. He stopped shivering and sweat dripped from his hat brim down his forehead.

The small rocks he sat on felt cold. He took one and pressed it against his injured side with the cold acting as a sort-of compress. It helped some. With his eyes closed, the sounds of the forest retreated.

A distant whistle answered him back.

Mina's phone buzzed. "Shoot," she said, interrupting the memories. "I'm so sorry, but I've got to go. My coworker's wife is having a baby."

Chapter 25

With another storm and a drop in the barometer, Deputy Clint Gallagher's wife had gone into labor six weeks early. Peter delivered the baby who had to be taken by helicopter to the closest children's hospital.

Mina officially graduated from ski instructor to deputy. Though she'd already been working as one on and off, when she put on her uniform and snapped on the radio and gun, a heaviness came over her. She spent the rest of her Christmas, patrolling the roads for partying drunks.

A few days later, she pushed open the door to the sheriff's office, grateful that the heat didn't blast her back. Each morning at 7:30, Sol insisted all on-duty personnel, including the deputies serving in other parts of the county and the on-call EMTs, speak on a group call.

Sol had already dialed the number into the conference line and waited for the others to join in.

"Hello." A voice emanated from the speaker and the meeting was on. No big updates. A slide-off was already cleaned up, the deputy down at the Junction had handled a domestic but no one would admit anything happened, and ski patrol had pulled a few passes from some very drunk guests, who wanted to start a fight over it. Typical day as Mina had come to learn.

After Sol hung up the phone, he and Mina sat down to go over their own day. He assigned her to patrol the highway within city limits for speeders. "Should be quiet today. Sometime in the next day or so I want you to go talk to your new buddy, Ryan."

"What for?"

"That group of Bigfoot hunters has made a camp in the vacant lot behind Outfitters. They've got permission, but I was over there last night and there's going on thirty of them, with more coming in. Groups like that make me uncomfortable."

"They are a bit out there."

"When you get a group like that, and I've seen it with something as simple as family reunions, they tend to have their own set of rules and leadership. Sometimes those rules clash with ours."

"Like the Orricks?"

"Exactly." The Orricks had family living in this town since before the mines opened and closed and would be here long after everyone else was dead. The family had long overflowed the borders of Lost Gorge. Many returned each Memorial weekend to the motherland for their family reunion.

Their last reunion had resulted in three arrests when at midnight they raced four-wheelers down the highway. Said they'd done it every year and nobody was going to tell them differently. Apparently, the previous sheriffs had given up and cordoned off the road for them. Sol didn't give up, and he and Mina spent every night dragging various members in to be arrested and then released the next morning. Good times.

"What do you want from me?" she asked.

"Go hang out with your friend. See if they have any plans to go look for Bigfoot and where. As trigger happy as people can be, I don't want them on private land or spooking folks."

"Ryan mentioned a bonfire tonight." They'd been casually texting.

"See, you are buddies. Use that."

* * *

A dark moonless night filled the valley as she pulled into the parking lot of Outfitters. She'd made a quick stop at home to change out of her uniform. When she worked the fair over the summer, she noticed folks can't relax around the uniform. A gap existed between her and the population everywhere she moved.

About five or so RVs were parked in a circle around a large bonfire. She imagined the numbers would hold steady until after New Year's when life would pull them home again. Several people moved around the edges of the light carrying mugs or plates of food. Ryan sat on a folding chair, eyes half-closed and legs propped up close enough to the fire he risked melting his shoes.

She sunk into an extra chair next to him. "Hey, your feet are going to be on fire soon."

He jerked up in surprise at her voice. "If only. What are you doing here?"

"I was driving home from work and saw the fire. Thought I'd say hello." She glanced around the flames at the standing figures. "Did I steal someone's seat?"

"No, it's been empty most of the night."

"How are the feet doing?"

"Peter said even if they heal, I'll always have trouble keeping them warm. The circulation doesn't come back." He stretched his legs. "This feels all right but night's the worst. I've taken to wrapping them up in a heated blanket."

Mina unconsciously pulled the scarf higher over her nose. It hadn't necessarily been a bad thing sitting in a patrol car for a good chunk of the week.

Ryan stood. "You want coffee or hot chocolate? We've even got cider. Warm you up."

"Cider sounds good." Before she could protest she could get it herself, he was off.

Philip, Ryan's friend, sat on a chair on the other side. "Good work keeping Ryan alive, and in one piece, considering he has all his toes."

"He kept me alive as well."

"Not the way he tells it. He said you kept him going when he would've sat down and called it." He grabbed a stick off the ground and poked a log in the fire, breaking it up. "Of course, he tends to take himself out of the stories. That's uncommon around here. Most of these folks come for the stories, making themselves and Squatch bigger with each telling."

"I have to ask. What's the difference between Sasquatch and Bigfoot?"

Phil leaned forward in his chair and whispered. "Careful, do you want to start a fight?"

"No, I just…"

He laughed. "I'm messing with you. Though, that is a common argument amongst us."

"Is there a difference?"

"Not really. Bigfoot was first coined in California when some loggers discovered footprints. Sasquatch came from the Native Americans. If anyone gets their underwear really bunched up about which term is right, they're probably posers anyway."

"Have you seen Sasquatch yet?" Mina asked, pulling her own eyes away from the fire to face the man.

"This trip? No. But ever? Still no."

"Why do it then?" She could sort of understand Ryan's quest as he truly believed he'd experienced something.

Phil leaned back in his chair and the legs sunk into the soot-covered snow. "That's the question, isn't it? Why are we all here chasing something that may not exist? And, if it does, we'll probably never see it."

"Especially if you're not sure."

"The short answer is, I don't know."

Mina liked this man, she decided, liked his forthrightness. "Bet that answer drives people nuts."

He laughed, a laugh that rolled from deep inside him. "It drives my kids nuts, that's for sure. They keep asking why I can't have a hobby like gardening."

"My parents say the same thing about skiing. 'Why you got to live in the frozen tundra jumping off cliffs?'"

"What do you tell them?"

Mina turned reflective. "I don't know," she said after a moment. "Just do." She wanted to change the subject to something lighter. "You don't look old enough to have grown kids."

"We started young. My wife passed when they were teens. When it was time for college, they both went out of state." Ashes and smoke blew from the fire. They adjusted their chairs accordingly. "Couldn't blame them for wanting to escape the sadness. I realized I did too, so I sold my company to take a few years off."

So much for talking about something lighter. "I'm so sorry."

"It happens. After that, I think I broke a little. I was always interested in myths and legends. One day I ran into Ryan flipping through a Sasquatch book at REI, and we started a conversation." He took a sip from his mug. "Told me about an upcoming trip, and I went along. Second I saw those prints, I was hooked. If my kids ask, I rented the house for the winter to ski, not hunt Sasquatch. They're coming to visit in a few days and should be here for almost two weeks."

Ryan walked back carrying two drinks and looking triumphant.

"Ryan, here." Phillip continued. "His search is more of an investigation and less of a need. Someday he may even walk away from it, if he finds what he's looking for."

"Sasquatch?" Mina asked.

"Validation."

Ryan reclaimed his seat on her other side. "Proselyting, Phillip? I don't think you'll convince Mina."

"I don't know, this one has the heart of a romantic, unlike you."

Mina turned to stare at the man she'd just met. Nobody had accused her of being a romantic. In fact, Patrick had argued she was the exact opposite after responding to his text calling her 'beautiful' as utter BS.

"What?" Ryan feigned offense. "I'm here, aren't I?"

"You're here, but a poet's soul you do not have."

"I can't argue with that." He propped his feet back up. "You ready for tomorrow?"

Mina perked up at the information she'd come for.

"I'm in," Phil said.

Mina sat straight up in her chair. "Ryan."

"What?"

The strident tone in her voice took her back as well as him. She hesitated. "It's just that with your feet and all." Who was she to tell him what to do?

She barely knew the guy.

"Maybe she's right," Phillip said. "Sit this one out."

"No, something's out there; I've got to look while we can."

"Not if one of your toes falls off," Mina muttered. "Where are you even going?"

"A friend has hired a snowmobile guide to take us into the mountains where there were some sightings years ago."

"Was the guide's last name Orrick?" Mina asked.

"Yeah, you know him. Is he trustworthy?" Ryan said.

"Enough, just hang on tight to the snowmobile. He'll get you there in plenty of time."

The talk shifted as other people joined the fire. Mina was content to lean back and learn what she could. Her cider grew cold as she sipped it.

Once there was a break in the conversation, Mina stood, she'd had an early morning. Ryan walked her to her Jeep, their breath creating a cloud that filled the space between them. "You really going to camp out," she said.

"You worried about me?" He nudged her with his hip.

"No," she said a little too sharply. "Seems a little risky is all." Even as she said the words, she wondered at herself for saying them. It pissed her off to no end when someone questioned the safety of her choices. Like they didn't think she was smart enough or capable enough to make good decisions.

"It is," he said without excuses. "But I'll take precautions, and I'll only go for one night."

"Sorry, it's your business. Have a good time."

They reached her Jeep, and she unzipped her jacket pocket to pull out her keys. "I'll see you later."

"Can later be Wednesday when I get back?"

Her brow furrowed. Was this a date or a friend thing? She felt a rush of panic. Was he interested in her? Had she inadvertently made him think she was interested in him? As a filler to the silence, she pushed the button on her keys and popped the locks. Wait, was *she* interested?

He waited for an answer with infuriating calm as if her response didn't matter much. "Yeah, I guess. You do owe me the rest of the story," she finally said. "Text me when you're down from the mountains."

He pulled open her door the rest of the way. "I'll do that."

As she drove away, Mina found herself smiling just a little when the headlights lit him up waving with a goofy smile.

Chapter 26

Ryan held on with an embarrassingly tight grip to the man driving the snowmobile. Mina had been correct with her warning about Sean Orrick and his driving skills.

Sean was quick to explain the slower the machine goes, the harder it is to control. "Needs the momentum," he'd explained, "to really bank the turns."

Any more momentum and Ryan would throw up. Once he realized he wouldn't die, or if he did it would be quick, he started to relax his clench.

They rode for about an hour up snowmobile trails marked with tall skinny poles. Mini replicas of the Cats used to groom the ski resort crawled along the trail, smoothing out the series of bumps the snowmobiles left.

Eventually, they ran out of level ground and the trail went up. Sean paused along the side of a mountain and killed the engine before pulling off his helmet, revealing a face mask where only his eyes and a tuft of red hair poked out. Ryan pulled off his own helmet, his head still vibrating from the roar of the machine. The two machines behind them, loaded with Squatchers and supplies, stopped as well.

"The trail gets bumpy and really tight around this corner. The groomers don't come past here." Sean said. "If you have a problem with heights, I suggest you close your eyes."

"I'll be all right."

"Sure, you will."

They started back up and the snowmobile crept around the blind corner. Ryan had lied. He now had a very big problem with heights.

The mountain fell away, leaving a trail only a few feet wide and a cliff hundreds of feet to the bottom. The machine itself took up the entire width of the trail and, at one spot, the right ski dangled over the edge. Ryan so wanted to close his eyes but they, along with the rest of his body, froze in place. As death came closer, he would see it coming.

This ungroomed part of the trail had a series of bumps and dips left from other sleds. Each time they dropped down a bump, the back track of the snowmobile slid back and forth. Ryan gripped the bars on the side until he realized if the machine slid, he didn't want to go with it. He tried to force himself to relax, but *force* and *relax* do not go together.

Fifty excruciating yards later, the trail widened. Sean pulled off and waited for the rest of the group to come around. "That gets the old heart pumping, doesn't it?"

Ryan didn't reply. He dismounted and sank into snow up to his knees, which concealed the fact his legs had no strength in them. Another machine came around the corner and pride kept him from laying prostrate on the snow offering thanks to God. His relief, however, was cut short when he realized that stretch of trail would have to be taken again on the way home. Maybe they could be helicoptered out, he half-seriously wondered.

They waited as the snowmobiles made it around the cliff: one carried Phil and the other Lane Jenkins, Bigfoot Hunter.

After another hour of driving, they came to an open field with untouched snow for at least an acre. At the opposite edge perched a forest with trees far too thick to ride through. Once they hit the open field, the other snowmobiles driven by Sean's brother and cousin, abandoned the single-file line to be side by side.

Sean revved his engine; its vibration running through Ryan. The others revved up as well.

He settled into his seat and yelled out to his guide. "If you're going to do this, win it."

The helmet nodded and before Ryan could draw his last breath, they were off.

The wind screamed past them. Phillip managed to wave from the back of his snowmobile as it passed them. Lane, however, hugged his driver so hard the man had to slow down to detach himself from the spider.

Sean let his brother and Phillip edge past them. As they moved far enough ahead, Sean and Ryan were in their blind spot, Sean gunned it at the last minute and passed some invisible finish line. He cut the engine next to the edge of the woods and ripped off his helmet, waving it in triumph.

Phillip and the brother came to a stop with a large amount of cursing from under the helmet.

"You'll never beat your younger brother, Dane," Sean said.

"I've beaten you plenty."

"Not today. It's only the last race that matters."

Phillip gasped for breath after removing his own helmet. "Think I left my lungs at the start. That was awesome."

The snowmobile with Lane slid in behind them; it pulled a sled with supplies and film equipment and ran slower. Once it stopped, a snow-covered Lane slipped off the side and lay in the snow.

The driver removed his own helmet and Ryan recognized him as Patrick, one of the rescuers who'd pulled them out of the canyon. He'd also seen him talking to Mina in a familiar way that bothered Ryan for a reason he couldn't identify.

Phillip stared at Lane. "Did you fall off?"

The prostrate figure couldn't answer; Patrick filled in. "Guy flipped out when I gunned it and about knocked me off the sled. I had to stop. Tried to tell him we wasn't racing because of the tow, but he said he'd walk in before he rode another minute."

"Thought he was going to walk across the lake through several feet of snow?" Sean scoffed.

Ryan hadn't realized the open field they'd raced across was a snow-covered lake.

Sean faced Lane. "You paid me to guide you in, but you also paid me to keep you safe. You endangered yourself and my man."

Lane tried to stand in the snow in an attempt to defend his dignity but only succeeded in falling back down. "He's a crazy driver. Could've killed me."

"He's my most cautious. You pull anything like that again, and I'll drive you straight down and hold onto the deposit.

"You wouldn't do that," Lane muttered as he dug himself out of the snow.

Sean stared him down until the TV personality finally muttered an apology. Sean, obviously not one to linger, moved on. "Strap on your snowshoes. The camp is about a quarter-mile through the trees down a hill. It's a lot more protected area, but we have to drag in our supplies."

Ryan's boot heaters and the walk kept the circulation going in his feet. Sean walked beside him, matching Ryan's shortened stride. "Heard you got frostbite." Despite the early afternoon sun, the shadows grew dark in the woods.

"Yeah, on my toes."

"I lost my pinky toe three winters ago. The circulation never is quite the same."

"That's heartening."

He laughed. "Figured, I'd give it to you straight. You boys really think you're going to find Bigfoot?"

Ryan resisted the urge to bend over to increase the temps on his boot heaters. "Probably not." He nodded toward the men following them at a growing distance. "Phil wouldn't know what to do if we did. It's the mystery of it, the chase for him. Lane would probably piss himself. He likes his sightings faked. Don't let him convince you to be on camera. A fool loves to make others look foolish."

"Thanks for the advice. What about you? What are you looking for?"

Ryan always had a pat answer about the scientific curiosity of it all, but he sensed in this man a sincerity lacking in others. "I've seen some things, some stuff I can't put words to. I'm just trying to figure it all out.

Sean pointed through the pines to a patch of aspens. "There's a bog in there where water comes up from the ground. I've got a hunting stand to watch the game come for a drink."

"Good spot."

"As long as my freezer is mostly full, I don't shoot—only watch. My wife thinks I'm a much worse hunter than I actually am. Sometimes it's easier to get out in the mountains if you have a reason, even if it ain't a good one."

The snow creaked beneath them with each step. Ryan's muscles tightened in protest, still recovering from their hike through the canyon. "One summer, I sat in a tree stand for two days straight. Only came down to pee," Ryan said. "Saw a mama wolf walk by with three pups. At that moment, I don't know if I would've traded seeing Bigfoot over them."

Sean stared over his shoulder to the patch of trees where his stand lay. "One night I was half-asleep or mostly I guess; it was coming on dawn." He paused.

Ryan didn't fill the space with the words he knew would come—the stories. Many of these mountain people had a story, one they hadn't told fully to anyone. Too afraid of being mocked or seen as less than. In his travels, he'd learned not to pry or prod. The story would come when the person was ready.

"Wasn't sure what woke me but I came to as if someone had jabbed me with a cattle prod." Sean started walking again and Ryan followed. "Then I heard the scream. Wasn't like anything I'd ever heard before, and I've been in these woods for forty years. Not a scream like in terror, more like a war cry. They do that?"

It took Ryan a second to realize he'd asked him a question. "Bigfoot? Yeah, they do." He thought back to that night in the rain when he'd heard that cry for the first time.

"Heard a thumping. Wasn't rhythmic like footsteps but like…"

Ryan resisted the urge to fill in the blanks for him. Too many searchers did that until a person couldn't tell what the original story had been and what was provided.

"I don't know…maybe something heavy falling. Then it stopped. I told myself it was an injured animal, but the next day I…. Hey, you won't tell nobody, will you?"

Ryan halted his steps so he could look the man right in his eye. "No, I won't. Not even the others."

Sean nodded. "Good." They picked up their pace and it was a good five minutes before he spoke again. "I found tracks later than morning. To anybody else, they would've looked like indentations in the mud but there was a pattern to them. A few looked like they had toes and a heel."

"Take a picture?"

"Nah. It wouldn't have come out that well in a photo, and most people would've thought I read too much into it. But I tell you what, I didn't go out hunting again that season. Wife thought I was dying, tried to get me to go to a doctor."

"How long ago was it?"

"Two years last fall. Whatever it was, I've never heard anything like it since."

* * *

They set up camp before dark, which was no easy feat considering how quickly night found its way this far north of the equator. The stars came out so thick and bright, it looked like they'd been smeared across the Milky Way, like butter on bread.

The Orricks and Patrick sat at the campfire with Ryan and Phil. Lane, cold and complaining, had already escaped to one of the tents and the relative warmth of a sleeping bag.

Dane and Sean teased each other until turning their attention to Patrick. "Heard, you're finally in love, Patrick. Who's the unlucky girl?" Dane said.

Patrick jerked up from where he'd been staring into the fire. "What? I'm not seeing anyone."

Even Ryan, who barely knew the man, could read the defensiveness in his tone. The Orricks had found a sensitive spot and were going to poke it.

"That's not the family rumor. Is it that Mina girl you brought around last year?"

Now it was Ryan's turn to jerk up, but nobody paid him any attention. "You mean Mina Park?" he asked.

"You know her?" Sean grabbed a log from a stack and tossed it on the fire, spreading sparks.

"No…barely." He turned the attention back to Patrick. "You dating her?"

Ryan didn't need the light of day to feel Patrick's glare on him.

"Didn't she break up with him?" Sean asked. "She always seemed too smart to fall for him."

For some reason Ryan refused to examine, he really wanted that to be true.

"It's not Mina; it's not anyone," Patrick growled. He stomped off to the trees, ending the conversation.

Ryan settled into his sleeping bag by nine after taking a rare pain pill. As the opioid relaxed his body and settled the burning pain in his foot, he contemplated the craziness of this adventure. Despite everything, it was a good decision to come to Lost Gorge.

The soft smile he went to sleep with disappeared when the scream awoke him.

Chapter 27

Mina yawned as she blew on her coffee. Why she bothered drinking it, she didn't know. It took hours for caffeine to kick-in to her body.

The early morning at the office was no accident as she wanted some time before their meeting and the responsibilities of the day to go over their John Doe report again. She clicked through the images of the scene on the desk computer twice before one caught her eye.

It was a close-up on the hand; the hand that had first signaled to her the presence of a body. She zoomed in on the left finger where a soft pale circle indicated where a wedding ring had been. Considering how intact she'd found the hand, Mina doubted it had come off in the attack.

A lot of the men in Lost Gorge didn't wear wedding rings consistently, but then again many of the women didn't either. Most of the married instructors had lost at least one ring from the constant taking on and off gloves. The ranchers worried about losing a finger in a baler.

She thought about the married people she knew and had never noticed a tan line as strong as the one on the dead man's hand.

He had worn his ring very regularly until he didn't. A cheater or a man recently separated? Nobody called to tell them they'd lost a husband. Maybe a divorced guy on a trip alone?

Sol came out of his office. "We've got a problem," he said before she could offer her new insight. "An SOS call came in from Sean Orrick's GPS. Said he needs a medical helicopter for a man with severe injuries."

Her finger hovered over the mouse while her stomach dropped. "Who?"

"He didn't say, but I have the coordinates."

Mina swallowed the plethora of words and panic that wanted to spill out. *Who was it? Were they all right?* Not only did she feel like she didn't have the right to ask the question, she knew there wouldn't be much of an answer. Not yet.

Sol moved to stand in front of a giant topographical map of the county pinned to the wall. She joined him as his fingers ran down the coordinates until stopping where the contour lines marking elevation ran the closest.

Whatever had happened, it had been in one of the most remote and rugged places in the county. "BLM land?" she asked.

"No, Forest Service." Which meant a combined rescue with federal employees, always a more complicated operation. The phone rang and Sol went to answer it while Mina stood on her tiptoes for a better view.

She ran her finger along one of the lines before stopping at a small body of water she had backpacked to a few times in previous summers. The trappers, in all their creativity, had named the water Spring Lake. What location had Ryan said they'd be going to? She glanced back to her phone lying on her desk but knew texting him would be pointless.

Sol returned to the room. "It's the Squatcher group," he said as if reading her mind. "That was Ellie Orrick. She got a text message from the GPS unit to send help. There's an injured man." Some GPS units came with a service plan that allowed for simple text messages to be sent.

"What now?" she finally asked.

"We're sending in a chopper." They shared a rescue chopper with two other counties. "In the meantime, you're going up with an EMT on snowmobiles. Sean's oldest is eighteen, and she knows the way. I'll come in on the chopper. That way one of us takes the fastest way in."

Mina debated asking if she could fly in but the chopper might take a few hours before it even arrived in Lost Gorge and seating would be limited. Hard to say which route would be the quickest.

In less than an hour, Mina stood at the trailhead outfitted in her best layers and carrying a helmet. She could drive a snowmobile as good as the next guy, but this trip required an advanced level better than that guy. A SAR guy road one machine with a sled behind it that could double as a stretcher, complete with a first-aid kit.

Sean Orrick's daughter, Kylie, a girl with equal parts freckles and pimples, shook Mina's hand as she approached. Mina couldn't tell if it was fear or nature for her to act the part of the grown-up, but Kylie's voice broke as she mentioned the text.

"If it had been your dad or your uncle hurt, they would've mentioned that in the text," she said. "They're too experienced for it to be them."

"It's like my dad to say he's okay when he's not." The fear and the freckles made her look twelve, and Mina wanted to hug her. "He wouldn't want us to worry. And my dad says, it doesn't matter how prepared and experienced you are, Mother Nature can be a bitch."

Another time and Mina would've laughed, especially after their trek through the canyon. "Focus on getting there. Everything else will take care of itself."

Mina mounted a machine behind Kylie as she led them up a trail only a true Lost Gorge native would ever consider passable and only an Orrick would attempt. Another day, it would've been one fun trip.

Once they climbed the cliffs, the snowmobile whipped across the white expanse. If she'd been able to peer over her driver's shoulder, she wouldn't be surprised to see 60 mph on the odometer. Definitely would've been a fun day under different circumstances.

By mid-morning, they slowed the machines and killed the engines. Kylie jumped off her snowmobile before it stopped completely as she launched herself into the arms of a man who stood waiting. Mina couldn't tell if it was her father or uncle but either way, something was wrong.

She knew the area well enough to know there was no way to land a helicopter or get a snowmobile into the campsite. Yet no sign of the injured man existed. She'd expected they would've dragged him out this far on a sled for pick up. That meant he was far too injured to move or already dead.

"What happened, Dad?" Kylie asked. "Everyone okay?"

Sean glanced at his tall but still so young daughter. Mina understood that look. How do I protect her from this? They could postpone the inevitable but they couldn't hide from it.

With that understanding, she reached out to shake Sean's hand with her mittens. "How bad is it?" Sean gave one last look at a girl, who may no longer be young by the end of the day.

"He died a few hours ago."

Mina's breath caught. *No,* she thought, *I didn't get him out of that canyon to die a week later.* "Who?" she whispered.

"His name is Phillip." Both she and the girl gasped but for opposite reasons. Kylie because she didn't know the dead and Mina because she did. "I already messaged Sol so he knows not to bother with the helicopter."

"What happened?" A list of causes ran through Mina's mind, from heart attack to buried in the snow.

"Kylie, unhook the sled and unload it. We need to drag it back to camp." The girl didn't argue; maybe she'd had enough time being an adult.

"Get your snowshoes on, and we'll walk in," he said to Mina. "Why don't you stay here with Kylie?" he called out to the member of SAR she rode in with. Why not, she thought bitterly, no one left to rescue.

She followed Sean into the woods. After they made it about twenty yards, she spoke. "What's going on? Why don't you want them with us?"

He glanced behind them to make sure they walked alone. "You're a deputy, right? Least you were in the summer."

"Yes, I am."

"Are you armed?"

Mina took a breath. "Yes."

"You better come see."

126

Chapter 28

Their location was far too remote to radio to Sol. Mina instead used Sean's GPS to send a message that the chopper would no longer be needed. Sol's return message was equally to the point. *Hold the scene; I'm on my way.*

"Where is the body?" She handed the GPS unit back to Sean.

"The camp is about a quarter-mile through the trees."

She followed him on a pair of snowshoes. "What happened?" He opened his mouth and closed it again; the right words not coming. "How'd he die?" she asked, trying to jump-start the conversation.

"I don't know but something ripped into him in the middle of the night. Something I can't…"

Now it was her turn to lose the words. She stopped and hunched over a bit, trying to force out the memories that always pried their way in. *You can't freak out, not now.* She straightened up. "Like before?"

He didn't have to ask what she meant. There had been no other topic of conversation for the last few weeks. Everyone knew the details despite, Sol's best efforts to hold onto them. "Maybe, but he wasn't…his body was sort of intact."

"Sort of?" The words tasted bitter on her tongue.

"His limbs weren't torn off just his insides, like gutting." Sean locked his jaw. His hands shook as he tucked the GPS into a pocket. Mina didn't need any more evidence of what waited for her. This was a man who feared God and nothing else.

"I know." And she did. "Anyone else hurt? Your family okay?"

The mention of his family was enough to settle him. "Only Phillip."

"You said he only died a few hours ago but how's that when the attack happened at night?"

"He held on." His voice broke. "For two hours, he kept hanging on. I knew the second I saw him we couldn't save him, but he kept breathing so I kept hoping. Thought maybe if we could get a helicopter."

"Did he say anything?"

"No. He was too far gone."

Mina thought about the kids he'd mentioned, coming in to spend the holiday with their only parent. "Was it an animal? Any tracks?"

He hesitated. "I don't know."

Only Sol rivaled Sean in his ability to track, and he knew these woods better than anyone. "You don't know?"

"Everyone trampled the area around his tent, freaking out and trying to help. We found him still tucked in his sleeping bag. Thing is, his tent wasn't damaged, and the sleeping bag wasn't ripped up at all."

"Wait, he was attacked in bed?"

"I don't know. Everything happened all at once. We heard a scream." He stopped, his eyes squeezed shut as if remembering. "The scream wasn't him; he would've been too hurt to make a sound but something, something ungodly was in those woods."

Mina could discount everyone else's story, but Sean made it a lot tougher. "Was he alone in the tent?"

Sean hesitated. "No, but I don't think...."

"Who was with him?"

"Ryan, his buddy. Nobody else."

Mina paused with one boot in the air before continuing their interminable walk. "Where's the body now?"

"Still in the tent. I knew there was no way he'd live if we moved him. We just did our best to keep him comfortable. After he passed, I had everyone leave his tent and told them to give it a wide berth. Figured you people would want to search it. Didn't want to risk messing anything up."

"But you saw the injuries."

"Yep, and I've never seen anything like them, and I hope to God I never do again."

"What did Ryan have to say?"

"Says he was asleep the entire time."

The four other men stood at Mina and Sean's approach, not out of respect or chivalry but out of obvious relief that somebody was here to do something.

The only problem was, she wasn't sure what she could do.

Working Search and Rescue was so much more straightforward. Somebody doesn't come home, she worked to bring them home. Mostly they came home alive and if they didn't, she knew why. All she felt capable of doing now was to sit on things until the people who knew something showed up.

Ryan didn't meet her eyes, but she ignored that for the time being. "Where's Phil?"

"I'll show you." Sean led her away from the fire where she could feel the eyes of everyone following her. She tried to straighten up.

"Stay in the previous tracks." She commanded. "I don't want to disturb the site more than it is." Several items from the tent—a backpack, a small cooler, and a sleeping cot—littered the ground around. She assumed this was to make way for the other men as they tended to an injured Phil.

Sean didn't argue. He stopped at the tent door and took a deep breath. "We did what we could."

She understood his guilt and wished she had a way to alleviate it, but she carried her own. "This isn't on you."

"When people hire me, it's my responsibility to bring them home safe."

"Let's do what we can to bring him home."

He unzipped the door of the canvas tent and pulled the flap back. Phil lay on the tent floor—rigor mortis had set in and frozen his face in his last gasp. Mina had stopped counting how many bodies she'd help recover. Not because there were so many but because it added up to an unbearable sum. She wanted to close Phil's eyes and mouth to make him look more peaceful but that would interfere with the investigation to come. She took off her mittens and replaced them with a thinner set of gloves.

With a moment's hesitation and an unspoken apology to Phil, she pulled back the sleeping bag. Had the discovery of the previous body not prepared her, she probably would've ended up in the bushes puking.

As it was, she closed her eyes and gave the nausea a moment to pass. Sean stood outside; she didn't blame him for not following her in. With the cold, the smell hadn't the chance to entrench the air around.

Whatever killed this man had shown no mercy or hesitation.

Mina left the tent to the comfort and fresh air of the forest. At the warmth of the fire, she pulled out her own GPS unit and synced it to her cell phone. It took a few minutes and a couple of tries until she had a signal.

We need crime scene analysis. I don't know what we have. The body is like before, although not in as bad of shape.

About ten minutes later she received a reply.

Ten-four. Lock down the scene and interview witnesses. Don't let them leave. Try to get a statement while it's still fresh.

Mina jumped to her feet. Dane was already getting a group together to walk out to the machines before dark. "I need everybody to hold up for just a few minutes."

Groans bounced off the trees.

"It won't be long." She glanced around. "Where's Patrick?"

The other men looked at each other. "He already went down," Dane finally offered. "Not long after you got here. Said you would take care of things, and he wanted to get word out." That left her alone to handle things, which she did not feel too prepared to do.

Lane, the documentary guy, paced the campsite, half muttering. Hard to believe she ever found him attractive.

"You, I talk to first," she said to Lane, wanting him away from the scene and her as quickly as possible.

Ryan stood at the edge of the fire, watching and waiting. She would talk to him last. It would be helpful to hear the others' stories first and see how well his lined up. She also wasn't quite prepared for a conversation with him.

She and Lane walked a way out from camp to sit on a couple of fallen trees, still uncovered and protected from the storms. Mina sat; Lane didn't.

"You sure we should be out here alone?" he asked, his gaze jumping from tree to tree to find that unseen attacker.

"I thought you'd be more excited to be this close to Bigfoot."

"Sasquatch," he said automatically. Realization seemed to dawn at what she said. "Of course. This will definitely feature in my documentary. I need to get my camera and get the scene with everyone's first impressions." He leaped to his feet.

Mina jumped in front of him. "No cameras. If I see one, I take it into evidence. You won't get it back until after the investigation."

He stopped and eyed her up, as if weighing her seriousness. "Fine. But if I'm going to talk, I need access to the site and interviews."

Mina had no authority to offer any of those things, which meant it didn't matter what she promised this guy. "Sure, as long you tell the truth. What happened last night?"

What happened to Lane hadn't been much. He'd struggled to get to sleep and was half-awake when he heard the scream. "I would've, of course, ran out to render aid, but the Orricks ordered me to stay behind."

"You just stayed in the tent, didn't help at all?" Mina tried and failed to keep the judgment out of her voice.

"Help how? Tell me what I was supposed to do. Couldn't call 911, couldn't run for help, couldn't fold all of his guts back in and sew him up."

Maybe he had done the most sensible thing. "Tell me about before the scream. You said you couldn't sleep. Did you hear anything before that?"

"I heard everything. I've been to comic-cons quieter. One time, I swear an animal or something rubbed against the tent. I could feel it push against the canvas."

"What did you do?"

"Woke up Patrick, but he said to go back to sleep, that it was probably a coyote or something." His stare at Mina held no question what he thought of that advice. "A coyote isn't nothing."

"How long was that before you heard the scream?"

"I don't know. The night went on forever."

"What about during the evening? Everyone getting along?"

"I guess."

"So, you just had dinner and crashed?" That had been Sean's description of the evening when they'd walked in together. He said it was too cold for much else.

"Yeah." He cocked his head. "Except for the night cameras."

"What cameras?"

"I always place a game camera with motion sensors. Phil helped me set it up; he was considering buying some and wanted to see how they worked."

Nobody had bothered to mention cameras. "Where?" Lane hesitated. Mina knew he wouldn't want to relinquish the footage. "If you want us to share with you, you need to share everything with us."

"I'll show you where."

Chapter 29

Ryan was used to people thinking he was crazy. What he wasn't used to was believing he might very well be on the slippery path to insanity.

He'd woken up next to a dying friend. They'd tried to stop the bleeding, but they soon realized all they could do was watch him die. For what felt like hours, he'd sat next to Phil as he bled out. He'd washed Phil's blood off his hands and face with snow melted over the fire but, like Lady Macbeth, the damn spot wouldn't leave him.

Would the sheriff allow him to call Phil's kids? He'd met them once when a family camp trip coincided with a sighting in Washington. They'd good-naturedly teased their father when Ryan had picked him up for a day of hunting. The kids, one boy and a girl, had booked a guided river rafting tour. Apparently, Phillip wasn't too fond of water, and they accused him of making up the sighting to get out of it.

What Phil was fond of, however, was those kids. He'd asked three times if they were sure it was okay if he didn't join them. As long as he bought beers and steaks at the end of the day, they said, all would be forgiven and forgotten. This day would never be forgotten.

Ryan kept his gaze on the coffee mug he held in his hand. Every time he looked up, he caught the stares of the others staring back at him, wondering.

At the sight of Mina following behind Lane, Ryan stood. She stopped short of him. Her dark eyes peered right at him as if warning him that no lie would be believed or tolerated.

"Let's talk," she said.

They walked away from camp to sit on a couple of fallen trees. Going by the tracks, this had been where the others had their interview.

"What happened?" she asked. Her tone brokered no familiarity. All the trust he'd earned had vanished.

Ryan wished she'd started with an easier question. "I don't know." She didn't respond, not accepting his attempt. The silence grew unbearable. "My feet were burning after the hike in. I took a couple of Percocet—more than I have before and fell asleep. When I woke up..."

He tried again, "When I woke up..." There weren't words that could describe the smell, the sounds of his friend dying a few feet beside him. "Sean was yelling, asking if we were okay. I turned on the lantern and Phil...he'd almost stop breathing. He'd gasp and then nothing for a few seconds. Each breath grew farther apart."

Mina reached out a hand to touch his knee but retracted it a few inches short. "Who opened the tent door, you or Sean?"

"Sean, I was focused on Phil."

"Did he unzip the tent door?"

Ryan thought for a minute before shaking his head. "I'm not sure, but Phil's sleeping bag was over him; I had to throw it off him. That's when I realized how bad it was."

"The sleeping bag wasn't zipped?"

"No."

"But you're sure he was under it."

"Yes."

"Ryan, how did you not—?"

"I don't know," he said, shoving himself up. "I don't know how my friend lay dying next to me and I didn't hear. I only took half a pain pill before, never two. It must've hit me hard."

"You woke up when Sean yelled, right? Do you think you would've heard anything if he'd been attacked in the tent?"

The tent where his friend lay was barely visible through the trees. "I only know what I saw when I woke up."

"What about the camera?"

"What camera?"

"Lane said he and Phil put out a motion sensor camera around the campsite just in case."

"He didn't last night."

"How do you know?"

"Because I told him not to bother."

Ryan had sat at the fire the previous night, wondering how much of a fool he'd been to trek through the forest with frostbitten toes. "He wanted me to help them. I told him Bigfoot never comes close to camp the first night. It takes a few evenings for their curiosity to get the better of them. Told him it was too cold and too dark, and we'd do it in the morning."

"And he agreed?"

Ryan clenched his eyes shut and pictured his friend asking him for help. "Said so. Then I drugged myself and didn't help him."

If he'd expected Mina to offer platitudes about this not being his fault, he would've been disappointed. She didn't and he wasn't; platitudes wouldn't ease his guilty conscious.

"How did you not wake up?"

That question again. When he was a kid, they'd asked him the same questions over and over—first the camp counselors, then the police, and finally his parents. He finally realized the questions wouldn't stop until they got an answer they liked, and the truth would never be that. Ryan stopped talking then and that seemed like a good strategy now.

"That's all I know."

She gave him a long look, and she couldn't have called him a liar better in actual words.

Chapter 30

After finishing her conversation with Ryan, Mina followed Lane's directions to where the camera had been set up. Sean accompanied her, but they left Lane back at the site to keep him from interfering. The camera lay on its side; knocked off its tripod.

Had Ryan lied to her about there not being a camera, hoping Lane would forget or not want to mention it? Or had he really believed he'd talked them out of it? But why would he? The entire point of the trip was to find Bigfoot.

"What do you want to do?" Sean asked.

His asking her that settled on her like a heavy sleeping bag. Like it or not, qualified or not; she was in charge of an investigation, at least for a few more hours.

"Bring me a clean plastic bag if you got it."

"I'll see what I can find."

She'd believed Ryan about the pills, believed him about sleeping through it. The pain in his eyes and guilt felt far too real. But the camera changed everything.

"Here." Sean had slipped through the trees and handed her a plastic grocery store bag. Not ideal but what they had. With her gloves still on, she slipped the camera into the bag, leaving the tripod to mark the spot. She'd taken several pictures of the site with her dying cell phone.

"I know that model. People use it for hunting," Sean said. "It has an SD card or a cord to plug it in. You won't be able to access the photos until you get to a device."

"How does it work?"

"It takes a series of pictures when it senses motion. Color shots during daylight and black and white at night."

"I didn't see any prints around here other than Lane's and Phil's original set." She tied the handles together on the bag. It was an outdoor camera and would hopefully survive the cold and wet. She didn't have much hope this would've caught the crime as they were a ways out from the tent.

"I've tried to keep everyone as close to the campsite as possible. I didn't want anyone ruining tracks before Sol could get here. Figured if there's something to find, he'll find it." To know Sol was to have complete trust in him, at least when it came to tracking.

That reminded her, however, of something she needed before anyone left.

Mina lacked paper or ink, but she had snow and sticks. In an area she cordoned off with a few logs, she had each man step into the snow and leave a print. With a small stick, she carved their first initial above each print. They would have to repeat it back at the station but at least when Sol arrived, they could map out who had gone where, except for Patrick.

* * *

Lane's cooperation ended, and he demanded to be taken down or he'd walk out. Nobody took his threats seriously, but Dane wanted to be rid of the man. Mina couldn't force them to stay beyond an arrest.

"Take him down," she told Dane, "but have some of your family keep an eye on him. I don't want him leaving town without us knowing." The freckled-face Orrick blood ran through much of Lost Gorge.

Sean and Dane returned to the snowmobiles—Dane to head down and Sean to make sure they got off all right. That left Ryan and Mina in the woods alone with a body.

They stood by the campfire as she pulled out some cookies and held them out to Ryan. "You want some?"

He stared at her a long moment before taking one out. "I didn't hurt my friend."

"Something did. You think it was Bigfoot?" She asked without irony, not

137

because she believed but he did.

"I don't know."

Mina looked down the darkening trail for about the thousandth time that day. The sun wouldn't last more than an hour, and she needed Sol to be here to pull her out of the deep end. Movement broke through the thick pines and unlike the previous 999 times, Sol walked through the trees, Sean leading the way.

Both men had hiked in with small sleds and supplies. "Where?" Sol asked by way of a hello, and she pointed to the tent.

Sean pulled off a pack and sank to a camp chair by the fire. "What a cluster this day is turning out to be." He noticed Ryan lingering by the fire.

"Like it or not, we'll all be spending the night. I'm not risking being on those trails in the dark. This day has seen a high enough death toll."

"Sol?" she asked.

"If Sean says it not safe, it's not safe."

She wondered if he'd stick to that argument once he understood exactly how involved Ryan was.

Ryan and Sean made some talk about warming up a few cans of stew while she and Sol went to the body. The temperatures were far colder than any morgue's storage, keeping Phil somewhat preserved.

They documented as much of the scene as the light would allow. She updated Sol on what she learned.

"So, Ryan's a suspect?" he said.

She bit her tongue against an argument she couldn't make. "If there's something to be suspected of. Thought I'd let you make the decision on what kind of attack this was."

He stood from where he'd been squatting next to the body, having just zipped it up in a body bag. They stepped out of the tent. "Mina," he said. "I'm sorry you're stuck in the middle of this. If I had known, I wouldn't have sent you. But you are here and our first priority is to that man in there and your second is to this office."

Mina never wanted to escape into the woods alone and unfettered more than she did at that moment. "I give you my word." She wouldn't run, and she wouldn't let him down.

Nobody slept much that night.

The four of them crowded together in one tent where every movement sent everyone on edge. They awoke before dawn, or at least that was when they finally gave up and got up.

Mina longed for a shower and a change of clothes, but she settled for a pee in the woods over a log. The cold against her hiney was enough motivation to hold it in as long as possible before the next one.

She stayed in Sol's tracks as they moved into the woods with untracked snow. "I want to do a circle of the campsite," Sol said. "I didn't dare do it in the darkness and mess something up."

"He wasn't attacked in the tent," Mina said. "Animal or man, there would've been a struggle and a lot more blood. Everybody said the tent was standing perfectly upright with the zipper partway open."

"So, somebody moved him, or he somehow made it back there?"

They started their search at the tent door. There were too many tracks and chewed-up ground to determine anything. They widened their search.

Twenty feet out they found a blood trail.

Red streaks followed along a set of prints that matched the winter boots on the body. Other than the blood, it would've been almost impossible to know this was the last path Phil walked. Several sets of tracks from different boots had come along the same way.

They photographed and marked the trail as the blood drops grew in diameter until they reached the source. Mina was very glad the others hadn't seen the spot where Phillip had lost his last battle.

Blood soaked the white snow, now a brownish red. An imprint in the snow, the size of a man, lay in the middle.

She squatted next to Sol as he examined the ground. She didn't need his commentary to know they looked at the spot where Phillip had laid, bleeding out. "How did he make it back?" she whispered. The site felt almost sacred.

"Probably instinct. I heard about a man who was stabbed in his bed, but police found him in the kitchen. There was a blood trail through the house and, near as they could figure, the victim was getting ready for work like a normal day. Didn't even try to call for help."

"Phil went back to his tent on instinct?"

"A place where he felt safe and protected, a place to die."

They searched the site for the tracks they hoped to find, a coyote or bear. "No Bigfoot prints this time," Mina said.

"Nope," he said without a trace of irony.

"Do you think Bigfoot is out there?"

"I think I know enough to know I don't know a lot. Do I believe there's an ape-man in the woods? No. Do I think there are things hidden out there that we have never seen and, if we did, couldn't explain? Yes. I've wandered these mountains enough to see and hear things I have no explanation for."

He gestured to the area they'd searched. "Although, I hope this doesn't turn into one of those things."

"When they first came, the Squatchers, I thought they were crazy," she said, looking back toward the camp where one of the craziest made breakfast.

"And now?"

"It's a bit romantic—if that's the right word—searching for something you'll probably never find but always keep hoping to." They stood about twenty feet from the blood on the snow. "I liked Phil. He had no guile—only the thrill of being in the mountains and living life."

Sol moved away from the bloody spot in an ever-widening circle. She followed him in his tracks until he put up a hand to stop. "There."

Next to a large pine tree, something had indented the snow in a vague shape of a footprint, a very large bare footprint. "No!" Mina said.

Sol squatted over it. "Nobody finds out about this until we know what's up. Nobody."

Chapter 31

The sheriff had sent Ryan and Sean down the trail as soon as dawn hit, leaving him and Mina alone to investigate. Abandoning her up there with something killing off people went against every instinct Ryan didn't know he had.

As if sensing his discomfort or at least sharing it, Sean spoke as they mounted the snowmobile. "They'll be okay. Sol knows these mountains better than anyone, and Mina is a lot more capable than most people born here."

The snowmobile ride back down didn't faze Ryan; the risk of falling off a cliff seemed like a fair trade for what they'd left behind.

When they stopped in the trailhead parking lot, Lane jumped out of a car, camera in hand. "I'd love to get your first reaction of the Sasquatch attack."

Ryan threw up a hand to block the light as well as the man.

Sean, who had more thought than Ryan's stunned response, jumped off the sled and pushed the camera away. Before Lane could react, Sean stalked off to pull down the ramp on the trailer.

Lane's attention turned to Ryan as he climbed off the seat. "Ryan, would you call this vindication? You've been talking for years about the dangers of Sasquatch. Now he's taken another life. If you would sit down for an interview—"

Ryan had always been slow to action. Had he been quicker in the woods that day as a child, maybe he could've saved a life.

He stood up from the snowmobile, his full height several inches above Lane. Without a word and before Lane saw it coming, Ryan grabbed the camera and ripped it from his hands. Using the metal rail of Sean's trailer, he bashed the side of it in again and again.

Still silent, he handed the camera back to Lane, who stood open-mouthed before he sputtered out a string of obscenities. Ryan walked away and climbed into Sean's truck. Lane turned his anger on Sean who replied, "Don't know what you're so pissy about. Your fault you dropped the camera in the snow."

Sean loaded the snowmobile onto the trailer before jumping in the truck. "What's his deal?"

"He wants to sell tickets to his show, and now we're the show."

"What do you mean?"

"He does a series of YouTube videos about Bigfoot hunting. I watched a few but they're pure BS. Most of his so-called evidence is invented."

"Where's his big money come from?"

"What big money?" Ryan asked. "The man lives out of his van for most of the summer."

"He offered me $5,000 for a two-day trip plus $5,000 if he caught something usable. I thought only a fool would turn down that kind of money. I got a daughter starting college next year."

"Turn the truck around," Ryan ordered. Fortunately, Sean chose to ignore the briskness, which probably wouldn't fly any other time, and turned around.

By the time they returned to the parking lot, Lane had fled, leaving nothing but tracks.

"He can't be that stupid," Ryan said more to himself. "Hurting Phil to make a better film. Nobody would believe him." That was something Ryan had first-hand knowledge of.

"Men do a lot of dumb stuff for the right price. I live on land that used to be a silver mine until it dried up. No less than four murders, that we know of, happened a hundred years ago. Some were my own kin."

Was it possible? Maybe it was more than possible. Six men went up, only one had a reason to murder. "Lane's not one to keep a secret when there's bragging to be had and a camera out. Looks like I'll be doing that interview after all."

Chapter 32

Keeping people from discovering secrets in a town as small as Lost Gorge and an internet with billions of users was difficult at best and impossible at worst.

While they were able to keep the knowledge of the tracks within the confines of the Sheriff's Office, the condition of the body made news before Sol and Mina got off the mountain.

Sol had sent Mina home to sleep that first night, where she did anything but.

The voices in her head would not stop their incessant jabbering, all demanding her attention. Her phone dinged around breakfast, and she grabbed it hoping for an update from Sol or something from Ryan. It was ski clients asking to book her for the week. They'd decided to extend their Christmas by a week and wondered if she was available.

She sent off a quick rejection and the name of three instructors desperate for work. With the sun coming up, she decided she was better off working than waiting and threw on her uniform.

Sol didn't look surprised when she walked into the office. "I called Clint off leave. We need him on this. Once he's done a prelim, we'll call the FBI again. They might show more interest in this case, as it was technically forest service land.

"Good. What do you want me to do?"

"Go back over the first guy. I want to see if there are any similarities, but I don't want to assume either way on whether they're connected."

Clint came out of the backroom, pulling off a pair of plastic gloves and dropping them in the garbage. Despite his training, he collapsed into a chair and put his head between his legs.

They both waited, understanding the horror he'd experienced.

Finally, Clint sat up and took a breath. "This one wasn't like before. The wounds were cut this time not torn, possibly a knife."

"His insides were pretty messed up." Mina would give anything to wipe that memory away.

"If it was a knife, it would've needed to be very sharp. Someone slashed him up and down, but they didn't stab him. There were also nicks on the bones."

"And on the other body, the bones were broken but not marked up."

Clint nodded. "Whatever it was, I don't think he saw it coming. There were no wounds to his hands; he still had his gloves on."

"He was wearing gloves?" Sol asked.

"Yeah."

"Meaning he had the time and inclination to put them on." Sol pondered on that. "Didn't jump out of bed in a panic. He was also fully dressed, but he could've slept in his clothes to stay warmer."

"Nobody remembered what he was wearing when I asked," Mina said. "Everybody else wore their clothes to bed just took off their outer layers."

"The question is," Sol said, "what enticed him out of the tent but not anyone else?"

"Could've been a coincidence. He gets up to pee and runs into a bear that decided to come out of hibernation." Mina didn't believe that but it seemed the simplest resolution to rule out. It was the answer everyone would want.

"I'm becoming less inclined to call these animal attacks, at least not until we've gone through every option. First one, we went into assuming an animal. This one, let's not assume until we have more. I'd rather think the worst and be wrong than walk around thinking we're safe."

"If it's murder, then what's the motive or the reasoning?" Clint asked.

"If it wasn't planned, then it could be Phil gets up in the middle of the night and walks into something he shouldn't," Mina said, thinking out loud. "If it was planned, it doesn't make sense the murderer would sit outside in the cold and dark all night waiting for the off-chance Phil decides to pee. They would've done something to entice him outside."

Sol wrapped his hands around his coffee mug and stared into its depths as if, like with tea leaves, he could divine. "What would've gotten him out of bed, not woken up anyone else, and not made him freak out.

"Bigfoot." Mina considered that thought for a moment. "Where's the camera?"

Chapter 33

Back at Phil's, where he was still staying, Ryan paced until his throbbing feet begged him to stop; then he paced some more. He picked up the phone to call Natalie, Phil's daughter. He dialed the number, but it took three tries before he could hit send.

She had questions he had no answers to. *How could he not have heard her father? How come her dad went out alone? Why had Ryan ever encouraged such an asinine hobby?* She hung up on him, leaving the last question echoing through his mind.

He'd told his so-called truth time and again without any thought to what people's responses would be. Good people had taken to the woods to find Bigfoot because he swore the beast existed. Some of them had no more outdoor experience than walking to their mailboxes.

Had he ever in all these years once discouraged someone from searching? No, because he was so sure he was right. Why didn't he tell Phillip to go home, to be with his kids who'd already lost a parent?

Ryan hung up the phone and called Lane. Much as he hated that man, he could know something. He just had to get the guy talking. As soon as Ryan said those magic words, *I'll sign a release,* Lane had him at the local hotel, camera ready.

"I want you to walk me through that day as much as you can remember," Lane said as the red light blinked record.

"You probably remember more about that than I do," Ryan said.

"No, not about this week. Before, when you were a kid."

It was one thing to tell fellow believers over a campfire when they were sharing their own tales, but to go on camera in front of countless people would open him up to ridicule that would follow him to every job, every home, and every relationship.

But if he wanted to get Lane talking, he'd have to give him something.

He told the first part of the story; the one rehearsed and repeated many times. But then he got to the part with her.

"Tell me, what condition did you find the body in?" Lane continued the barrage. "Was Bigfoot eating her? Could you see blood?" Lane didn't even try to hide the salaciousness in his voice.

"Hannah." Ryan closed his eyes and pictured the counselor who'd welcomed him with a smile.

"What?"

"Her name was Hannah."

He'd been fourteen and all of the sudden he got girls for the first time. He'd literally squeaked out a hello when meeting her. The other boys bragged about what they would do with her given the chance. Boys who knew way more things than Ryan. It wouldn't be the last time he'd wonder what his parents had been thinking when sending him there.

"Was she pretty?" Lane pressed. "Was she friendly with *all* the boys?"

Parts of the story had remained untold, a lot of the parts that included Hannah. He'd never met her parents and had no idea what they thought of him, but he could assume the worse. This would bring it back to them again.

Could he sacrifice one victim to help another?

"I saw she was already dead and went for help." Ryan truncated the story; Hannah would remain in the past. He stood, yanking the mic off his shirt.

"No," Lane said. "I need more than that. I need the good stuff."

Ryan glared "Sorry, your YouTube viewers will have to find something else to watch."

"It's not YouTube," Lane yelled. "It's Netflix, and it's a freaking million if I can get footage of Sasquatch."

Ryan laughed. "Seriously? Good luck with that. We've been at it for years."

"I know, but this will be so much better. A murdering beast sells more than a gentle giant."

Ryan had never hit anyone before, never had the need. The shocked gasp on Lane's face as Ryan's fist punched straight into Lane's gut matched Ryan's own surprise.

Lane slumped to the ground, sucking in air and adding a touch of the dramatic. Always the showman.

"Did you hurt Phil?" Ryan yelled. "Did you murder a good man to sell tickets to a show?"

Lane turned up a stricken face. "No, of course not. But don't fault me for capitalizing on an opportunity you are all too stupid and too superstitious to take."

Ryan wished he was the kind of man to kick another while he was down.

Punching this guy wouldn't give him the answers he needed, but he had another option.

After kicking Lane out, he made a phone call. "Sean, I need to get back to that campsite. Can I rent a snowmobile from you?"

Ryan had to pull the phone away from his ear as his response included an unnecessary amount of yelling and cursing ending with, "You want to get yourself killed?"

"I need to know what happened that night. How a friend could be butchered while I slept two feet away."

"What do you think you can do the police can't?" he asked.

"I've been tracking Bigfoot for almost twenty years. I know his signs and, more than that, I know what isn't him. The police will be looking at everything but a monster."

Silence filled the line.

"And if it wasn't a monster," Ryan continued. "I'm fairly sure who it was, and I know his track as well."

"I'll take you. We leave before first light, and we return before dark."

"You could drop me off and pick me up the next day."

"I was responsible for Phillip's safety. He hired me to guide him up and down, and I failed him. Least I can do is figure out what happened. I'll pick you up tomorrow.

Ryan needed to talk to one other person before he could face the mountain.

149

Chapter 34

Patrick walked through the sheriff's office door carrying a pair of boots in his hand. "Sol around?"

Mina stuffed down her irritation at him for leaving her at the camp to handle it. "In his office. What's up?"

"He wanted to see my boots." He held up an almost new pair of Sorel black boots.

"Another season, another new pair, I see." There were guys who duct-taped their gear together, then there was Patrick.

"Good gear, good outcomes."

She rolled her eyes as she yelled for Sol. He came out of his office with no welcome smile for Patrick. "I shouldn't have had to ask you to bring these over."

Sol's tone had always been Switzerland, never revealing an emotion from one extreme to another. Mina glanced at her computer and clicked to open the first thing she saw, not wanting to be a part of this.

"I told you when we met on the trail I needed to get down," Patrick said.

"And I told you to go back up until we could retrieve the body."

Patrick dropped the boots on the floor with a clump. "Have a good one, Mina."

She didn't look up from her screen where she'd inadvertently opened the photos of the first body. With all the chaos, she'd forgotten about the wedding ring or lack thereof.

Mina stared at the hand of a recently single man when a vague recollection popped into her brain. Adrienne's missing date was divorced. Without anything resembling a lead, Mina looked up the employee directory on her phone and found the number. Adrienne picked up on the first ring. "Hello."

"Hey, it's Mina. That guy who stood you up, you remember his name?"

"Girl, I make it a point to only remember the names of the guys who show."

Mina couldn't argue with that sound logic. "I don't suppose you still have his number?"

"Sure, it's on my phone. I'll send it over."

Just as her phone dinged the answer, Sol opened the door. He stomped his feet with a ferocity, unusual for him.

"What's up?" she asked.

"Your boy, Ryan, is out in the parking lot wanting to talk to you."

So many emotions reacted to that statement, Mina would need an hour to sort all through them. "Why?" She didn't have an hour.

"He said he wanted to see how you were doing." Sol pulled his sheriff's cap off. "Look, I don't have to tell you to keep your distance while we're sorting this all out."

But you just did, Mina silently added.

"Talk to him, keep it professional, and see if he has anything else to add."

She slipped on her coat and was out the door before Sol could offer any more advice.

Chapter 35

Ryan wanted to see Mina one more time before they headed up the mountain. Also wanted to get her thoughts on everything that had happened but knew those wouldn't be had for a penny. He stood in the snow and cold outside the office, not wanting to go in.

She stepped out the door, zipping up a uniform coat several sizes too big for her. The makers of the uniform had obviously not pictured a deputy of her size when designing it.

"Hey," he said. "I wanted to see how you're doing."

Her expression let him know what a dumb question that was. "How are you doing?" she asked.

"Not good." He tried to keep the emotion out of his voice but couldn't and stopped speaking at that statement.

She gestured to his car. "Let's climb in before we both lose a limb."

He started the engine and the hot air blew out. He wondered how long until he wasn't so appreciative of the miracle of heat. "I called Phil's daughter." Mina didn't respond, and he rushed to fill the silence. "I had to. He was there because of me, because he believed my story. I shouldn't have kept this going. I should've forgotten everything I saw that day and listened to my therapist when she said I imagined the whole thing because of trauma."

"Did you imagine it?"

"No, but it would've been better just to accept that answer and move on."

"Ryan, what are you holding back? You haven't been straight with me from the get-go."

He clenched the steering wheel, wishing he was anywhere but having this

152

conversation. "The girl I found, who'd been attacked, she was still alive."

"You said you found a body."

"Not at first. I heard her crying out for help, and I found her in a bog surrounded by reeds several feet deep. Blood dyed everything red." Ryan could still picture the green weeds looking like their bottoms had been dipped in paint.

"She said something had come out of the trees and attacked her, a bear maybe. Whatever it was, it got distracted and ran off. I had a first-aid kit with a few Band-Aids, and I stupidly pulled it out. Like I could somehow put her intestines back into her body."

Mina reached out a hand like she wanted to take his but hesitated and instead let it sit a few inches away.

"I heard this godawful scream in the woods, not a bear but an enraged beast in a fury. And I ran."

"What made you so sure it was Bigfoot?"

"I saw it. I stopped and turned at the edge of the clearing. It strode out of the trees on two feet; arms hanging down. For a split second, I thought someone had come to rescue us. But as it came out of the trees, I could see black hair covering its entire body. Every part of me shook. He screamed one more time, and I ran."

He sucked in a breath. "Didn't matter I was hurt, didn't matter it was almost dark, and it didn't matter that I left her behind."

"You were a kid," she whispered.

"I was a coward, who spent the night hiding under some bushes. I found the meadow at dawn, but by that time, there wasn't much of her left. A few hours later, I finally stumbled into a search group from the camp. I lied; told them she was already dead."

"Ryan, I..." Mina couldn't think of words.

Ryan straightened, wanting to change the subject to something more concrete. "Have you made any progress on Phil?"

Her hand retreated. "We're doing everything we can."

"I've tried to remember something, anything before the scream."

"How well did you know him?"

"I know who he is now, but I don't know much about his old life."

"What does that mean?" she asked.

"The CEO/corporate him. I stayed with him once in Seattle, and we went out to dinner. Everyone knew him, wanted to talk to him. The restaurant put him at the head of the list. Not like my quiet guy hiking buddy. When this gets out," Ryan said, "it's going to be big news."

"We're still trying to process the crime scene and the body to understand that night," she said. "We don't have the resources to—" She cut herself off with a glance at Ryan.

"You're not going back up there, are you?" Ryan asked. He knew the sheriff wouldn't look too favorably on him and Sean heading up.

"No, we worked pretty fast to get what we needed. Couldn't risk losing anything to the elements." She grabbed the door handle. "I should go."

"I understand."

She held onto the handle without pulling it. "Ryan, people are going to be suspicious about how many bodies you've been around. Be careful what you say." Without another word, she pushed open the door and jumped out before he could respond.

He noticed she didn't say whether she was one of those people.

With Mina's confirmation they had finished with the crime scene, he called Sean to tell him they were good to go. Ryan tried to ignore the guilt of not being entirely honest with Mina.

Chapter 36

When Mina had first met Ryan, she regarded him as no one who'd fit in at Lost Gorge and by extension her kind of life. When he looked up at her as she came out of the office, she almost didn't recognize him.

She tried to sort out what had changed—his beard had grown in thick and darker than his hair, he wore the ball cap all local men had to wear, but he also carried a sadness whereas before he'd seemed almost childlike in his excitement.

When she relayed to Sol the contents of the conversation, she left out the last part.

"Find out everything you can about Phillip," Sol said. "We need to know the big players in his life and who benefits from his death. When I called to inform his kids, they weren't in a position to quiz. Once we know more, we'll be in a position to ask the right questions."

After reading enough about Phil Griffith to know he was smarter and more successful than about 99.9 percent of the population—other than the whole chasing Bigfoot thing—Mina needed something to distract her. Men like him shouldn't die alone in the woods.

She searched the phone number of Adrienne's date. The name tied to the number was Grayson Moore. A glimpse into social media accounts under that name showed that Grayson hadn't lied about his occupation. Mina found links to his articles about everything from scaling Denali to rafting the Nile in Uganda. She liked this guy's style.

Odd though, a reporter on scene the very day of an attack, and yet she didn't see any articles about Lost Gorge. She thumbed through his Twitter feed; he hadn't posted in two weeks. He did post the day after the attack—about heading to Africa for the holidays.

Mina called his number again. It went straight to voicemail without a ring like it had a dead battery.

He'd posted every other day but nothing for the last two weeks. He told Adrienne he'd be offline, but it wasn't like Africa was the moon; they had Internet.

Something about his last Tweet didn't sit right. Mina stood up to pour herself another cup of coffee. The pot had run dry so she put another on. As it percolated, so did she.

Africa, that's what bothered her. The man appeared to be a worldwide traveler; he wouldn't say he was going to an entire continent. He'd mention a specific country or city.

What was she saying? Someone killed him and posted from his phone? That felt far-fetched even for an investigation that included Bigfoot as a suspect.

The coffee maker sputtered out its brown liquid into the pot. *Cate,* that's who she needed to call. If a reporter was doing a story on Lost Gorge, they would've reached out to Cate, who would welcome all PR for the town.

Cate answered on the first ring. "Mina, I'm so glad you called. James has wanted you and Ryan to come for dinner for the last week but every time he asks Ryan, he's off to the mountains."

"It's been a crazy time."

"What about tonight? We'll keep it short, but you've got to eat. You wouldn't believe the amount of food simmering on my stove."

"Will Ryan be there?"

"No, I've given up on that man."

Mina swallowed the knee jerk no. She had to talk to Cate, and she had to eat. "What time?"

* * *

The twins, unused to having company, about tackled Mina as she walked through the door vying for her attention. "Want to see my room?" Chris asked.

"No, she doesn't." Kelly wrapped her arms around Mina's waist. "Your room is smelly; she's going to mine."

"Shut up."

Mina jumped in before the fight could explode. "I will see both your rooms." Chris raced down the hall as she leaned over to Kelly and whispered, "I'll hold my breath."

Kelly took her hand, and they walked down together. Chris was already jumping on his surprisingly made bed. "Look how high I can go."

Mina, an only child, didn't fully understand men until she'd started teaching little boys. Apparently, the need to show off is ingrained from birth. "You want your mom to yell at the both of us?"

The jumps immediately stopped. "Don't tell, okay."

"Okay."

Cate found them in Kelly's room and managed to convince the kids it really was dinner time. James was already sitting, oblivious to Cate dishing out food and corralling the kids.

"How are you doing?" Mina asked as she found a chair, the kids on either side of her.

"Oh, I'm fine thanks to you," James said.

Cate took his hand with a loving gaze. "It's going to definitely be a new year for us."

Mina was due back at the office as it was her turn to work the night shift. She didn't want to talk in front of the kids but couldn't stand to lose her window. "Cate, did a man named Grayson Moore ever contact you about doing a story on Lost Gorge?"

Cate stopped dishing broccoli to Chris, spoon in hand. "Grayson? I'm not sure. I get calls from freelancers all the time wanting to do stories." She sat back down. "Most of them are bloggers with five followers looking for free passes and lodging."

"You would've wanted to work with this guy. He was legit, wrote for a lot of the big travel and outdoor magazines."

Cate looked to James as if he could source an answer, but he didn't offer one. "Why do you ask?" she said.

"He was around the day…" She glanced at the kids who paid more attention to wrapping noodles on their forks than the adult conversation. "…the day everything happened on the mountain." With extra ears at the table, Mina went with a lie that could be a truth. "I heard he was taking some pictures and thought he might've caught something."

Cate nodded. "I'll go back through my emails. I know I sent out several press passes three or four months ago when I did a big campaign."

"Thanks, I reached out to him on Twitter, but it doesn't look like he's there a lot." Dinner went on, and they moved to talking about Lost Gorge's favorite subject—the weather and when it would snow again.

After dinner, Mina climbed into her Jeep but before she could turn the key, she remembered another reason she'd come tonight. Chris had complained about his ski boots pinching during their last lesson, and Cate had called in with a credit card to the resort to buy new ones. They'd left the old pair behind, and Mina had been meaning to return them.

She made her way back to the front door with boots in hand. James's voice carried through the door. "Maybe you should stop making friends with so many people."

Cate answered back, but her calm voice didn't come through.

"Kids, go to your room," James yelled.

Mina pushed open the door to slip the boots inside. The open door of a closet was only a foot away.

"Do you even want me here?" James asked. His tone was more of a question than a demand.

"Of course, I do," Cate answered.

The coat closet was filled with enough winter clothes to outfit the Olympic village. Mina set the boots down between a little pair of pink boots and a pair of men's black Sorels. James's voice carried again, and Kelly began to cry.

She slipped out the door and to her Jeep, more worried about Cate and the kids than the emails. She would keep a closer eye on the family.

Chapter 37

Ryan helped Sean unload the single snowmobile from the back of his truck. "Figured you wouldn't want to drive your own," Sean said.

"Not on this trail."

They sped up the trail without stopping. Both were determined to get to the camp and back before darkness would sweep through the forest. It had to be that day. Another storm threatened in the coming days and would wipe out any signs.

The Orricks had hauled out all the gear from the site, leaving only trampled snow. Ryan and Sean stood where Ryan and Phil's tent had been.

"I'll walk out there," Sean said. "You don't need to."

Ryan didn't have to ask where he meant. "I need to see it, need to get it over with. If there are any tracks or signs to be found that'll be where it is."

"What exactly are you hoping to find?"

"Lane said he placed one camera and handed it over. Knowing that guy, I can't imagine he'd give up everything. He had to have placed another camera and in a better position."

Ryan made a 360, scanning the area for possible sites. A thick pine tree taller than the surrounding ones overlooked an open area—the area he'd been avoiding.

"That way." He pointed. Sean followed, neither one of them speaking.

The blood had settled into the snow, leaving it a yellow pinkish hue. The sun shone, a blinding brilliance that belittled the deadliness of the spot. Several sets of footprints from both the campers and Mina and the police littered the area.

Sean hunched over the tracks while Ryan scanned for a good spot for the camera. "I think we all came down this path at least once that night to pee," Sean said.

"That could be another reason Lane and Phil would place a camera here. The scent could draw out something not happy about his territory being invaded."

Sean cocked his head to one side. "I see everyone's tracks but yours."

Ryan didn't much like the questioning tone in his voice. "As knocked out as I was, I would've peed my sleeping bag before getting up at night."

"Sure." Sean didn't sound sure.

Ryan ignored him and worked his way through the brush surrounding the trees. In the summer this brush would be several feet tall, now it only went to his knees. A flash of red, much brighter than the remaining blood, caught his eye. Two apples sat on the snow; a lure set by Phil.

Ryan glanced above him. A small camera nestled in the branches pointed down at him—a camera set up to take pictures at any movement. He stood on his tiptoes and pulled it down, flipping open the side door to reveal the SD card.

Maybe, just maybe, it had caught what destroyed Phil.

Before he could call out his discovery, Sean yelled back with one of his own. "Ryan, come look at this." His voice held a hint of panic.

Ryan trudged through the snow, the bushes pulling at the fabric of his jacket. Sean squatted over the snow about twenty feet from the blood. "What is it?" Ryan asked.

He didn't respond, only pointed. Ryan leaned over, his eyes following Sean's gesture. At one glance, he took a step back, his hand covering his beard. A bare footprint, twice the size of any he left, was perfectly etched in the snow.

Ryan retreated farther back.

"You think this is legit?" Sean demanded. "Should we use that plaster you brought to get a mold?"

It wasn't the sight of the print that freaked him out. Twenty years at this, he'd seen his share of Bigfoot prints. Not today, he thought. He didn't want to see one today. Seeing that would prove he'd led Phil to his demise.

"What do you think?" Sean asked, unaware of Ryan's quagmire. "Could be proof something else was out here besides us." He would want to believe anything besides a human had been responsible for this disaster.

Ryan grabbed onto a nearby branch, using it to ground himself. "Let me look closer." He took a deep breath and forced himself to return to the print. If he was to blame, he'd own it. He squatted over the print.

Right away, something seemed wrong. He pulled a magnifying glass out and leaned forward even more, analyzing the contours of the foot.

He rolled onto his heels and stood. "It wasn't Bigfoot. And it definitely wasn't animal."

"How do you know?"

"It's a fake. Somebody wanted this to look like a Bigfoot attack." Ryan fingered the camera in his pocket, wondering if he had their picture.

"Why? It's not like the sheriff would buy that and stop investigating."

Lane had worked hard to earn his money.

Chapter 38

Who was Grayson Moore?

Mina began the day at the office staring at his face on Twitter and searching for anyone who knew him. She'd called the magazine that had published some of his articles, but their dealings with him had been through email, which they provided an address for. She sent off a message asking him to contact her.

A background check didn't find any criminal history, but he did have a sister.

A soft voice answered the phone. Mina told the sister the same story she'd told Cate. That Grayson had been in town the day of an "incident" and she wanted to speak to him, see if he'd witnessed anything.

"I haven't talked with him in a month," the sister said. "We talked more when he lived in New York, but not as much since he went off the grid a few years or so ago."

"What do you mean 'went off the grid'?"

"He was a financial reporter, freelancing with the *Wall Street Journal* and some others. Then one day, he got tired of it and became some sort of travel/adventure reporter. He's been hard to keep track of ever since." The sister called out to someone to be quiet, she was on the phone. "Why are you looking for him again?"

"We're investigating an incident at our ski resort. I found out he was there the same day. I thought with him being a reporter, he might've seen something others had missed."

"I get it. We once walked down Fifth Avenue and some guy was pickpocketing this woman. I didn't notice; even she didn't notice. But he saw it and stopped it. Nothing gets past him."

"I tried his phone, but it goes straight to voicemail," Mina said. "His Twitter account said he's in Africa, and I thought maybe you'd know a way to get a hold of him." Silence filled the line. "Ma'am?"

"No, that's not right. He wasn't going to Zimbabwe until June. The kids and I were going....Hold on." The clicking of the laptop keys proved she was double-checking Mina's answer. The voice that came back no longer held the tired frustration of a little sister. "He always calls at Christmas. I thought maybe he was a few days late. I've been worried..." Her voice quivered from far away. "Where did you say you were?"

Mina needed a life jacket for this depth. "Hold on a second; I'll get you the sheriff." It would take all of two seconds to Google Lost Gorge and find out what "incident" had occurred a few weeks ago.

She grabbed Sol in his office, gave him a very quick summary, and pressed the phone in his hand.

He took the call in his office, and Mina waited outside.

It took a second after Sol's goodbye for him to call her into his office. He sat behind his desk covered with photos of Phil's crime scene.

"What have you been up to?"

His voice was even, but he still gripped the phone.

She told him about Adrienne. "I learned about him right before the call for Phil came in. I put it aside and then started calling around yesterday after looking up Phil's past."

"Mina, you can't go off on your own and not tell me."

"I didn't go off; I made some phone calls ten feet away." She was thirty-two years old and didn't need her hand held.

"This isn't like your other jobs. You can't do your own thing and check in now and then. I may have just told a woman her brother is dead, and I don't know that and nor do you."

Her entire body clenched down to her toes. Maybe she should've said something sooner, but she was new at this. "You're the one who wanted me to take this job."

"I wanted you because you're smart, and you will do anything to save someone. But you can't do it by yourself."

Part of her wanted to walk. This wasn't her idea. Wasn't she only doing this as a favor? But a growing part of her needed to see this through, needed to know she hadn't completely failed the missing man.

"Fine," she said.

Sol, never to dwell once he said his piece, gestured to the photos of the crime scene on his desk. "Almost everyone's tracks show up between the tent and the crime scene except Ryan's—"

"Could be because he went to bed so much earlier than the rest and was so out of it." She regretted that quick and very biased response immediately. "Sorry, we should look at all options."

"I also need you to call Patrick to come in. I have some questions for him."

"About what?"

Sol pulled out a single photo and handed it to her. "What do you see?"

What she saw wasn't in question. It's why she saw it she had no answer for. Patrick's boot print in blood.

* * *

Patrick sat across from Sol and Mina. In any other sheriff's office, someone who didn't know the suspects would do the investigating. With the second death happening on public land, they could call in the FBI. The FBI, however, was still deliberating cause of death and wasn't in a hurry to jump into "animal attacks."

They'd pulled Patrick off the mountain mid-shift and sat him at Sol's desk still wearing his black ski pants with his coat thrown over the back. They didn't have an interrogation room but probably wouldn't use it if they did. Sol wanted to go at this at a friendly level, to start with.

"Walk us through the night again?" Sol asked Patrick.

Mina stared at the man she'd known for more than a few years and wondered if she knew him at all. She knew his family, everyone knew the Orricks, but only in the way she knew everyone else in town. She knew his passions but only because she shared them. She knew his dreams but…no, she didn't really.

She wanted so much for there to be some innocent reason, but that realization made her recognize her own biases. At that moment, guilt or innocent, she knew she could never trust this man again.

"You never left the tent?" Sol asked as Patrick finished his recitation, not that much had changed since his first one.

"Not after 11 or so." He bounced his foot on his knee. This was Mina's first interrogation, and she hunted for some sign of lie or truth.

Sol laid out the photo of the footprint in the blood. "That matches your print."

Patrick leaned over the photo. "Okay." He sat back; his expression unchanged. "I imagine all of us walked through his blood at some point in the morning."

Mina wondered at his lack of emotion. Was it his training or something else that kept him so sedate?

"Except this wasn't by the tent. It was where someone attacked Phil." Sol emphasized the word 'someone.'

Patrick's foot dropped to the floor. "I never saw where it happened. Sean didn't let any of us wander around."

"So how did your print end up in the blood?"

"Where did you find it?" While Sol's voice remained even, Patrick's went up a notch, or two.

Sol described the large tree and the small open area surrounded by high bushes.

"Oh, that's easy." Relief washed through Patrick as he relaxed in the chair. "That's where I peed the night before. I think all of us did. He must have bled into our footprints."

"He did on a few," Sol said nodding. "But here's the thing, when your tracks walked away, they made a trail of blood." He set out another photo. "You can see here, the tracks get more faded as they go. You walked on his blood."

"That's bull. I didn't kill that man; I barely knew him."

"I didn't say you killed him. I said we found traces of blood on your boots.

Patrick, tell me something that makes sense."

"I don't know. Maybe I went out to pee after he'd already returned to the tent."

"You just told me you never left your tent."

"Come on, I could've done that half asleep. I've peed in the laundry hamper after having a few too many. Didn't know I'd done it until the smell got to me."

Now the panic in his voice grew. Mina stared at her hands, the hands he'd once rubbed the cold out of one night snowshoeing under the moon.

"Mina," Patrick said, as if reading her thoughts. "You know I didn't do this."

"We have to ask these questions," she said in an almost whisper. She took a deep breath. "And you need better answers." This came out louder.

Patrick pushed to his feet, almost knocking over the chair as it teetered back down. "You arresting me?"

"No," Sol said, shoving his hat back. "You can leave, but we'll have more questions."

Patrick left them sitting there. "There's no motive," Mina said after a minute as she moved from beside Sol to across from him.

"Not that we know of, but we don't know everything."

"Are you sure about the tracks?" Even as she asked, she knew it was a stupid question.

"Those tracks were all over the scene, before and after Phil had been killed. If Patrick had gotten up to pee half-asleep, he would've done it a lot closer to the tent and not wandered around."

"I just can't wrap—"

Outside the window, Patrick yelled something indiscernible and a few choice cuss words that weren't. Mina jumped to her feet and went to the window. One glance and she ran to the door, yelling back at Sol. "He's going to beat the crap out of him."

Chapter 39

Ryan and Sean drove straight from the trailhead to the sheriff's office. Ryan had made a plaster mold of the footprint as proof.

He stepped out of Sean's truck and reached for the back door where the mold sat. Something slammed into him from behind, smashing his head into the window. For a second, he had the crazy thought Bigfoot had finally got him.

As he fell to the ground, he rolled over and put his hands up to deflect. The man from the campsite, Patrick, jumped on him fists out. "You murdered that guy, you crazy effer. Tell them."

Height was about the only thing Ryan had going for him. He shot his hips up, pushing Patrick off balance and bent his legs to his head. He crossed them in front of his assailant and rolled forward, pushing him to the snow.

Patrick scrambled out and pulled back his fist as Sean tackled him with the sheriff following. Mina pulled out a pair of handcuffs, but Patrick still flailed his hands flying in every which way.

Ryan jumped up without thinking and ran to grab another arm before Mina could get hit.

Within a minute, Patrick had been cuffed to the railing of the stairs. Anger still rolled through him as he cussed at Ryan and everyone else. "He did it," he screamed. He turned to his uncle. "You know I didn't do this."

"Then shut up," Sean yelled back, his face the same shade of red as his nephew. "You're looking capable of murder right now."

"He was alone in the tent next to a dying guy." Patrick's voice went a few notes lower as he swallowed his rage. "I was with you and Dane the entire night; you know I didn't do this."

"I know."

Did he know or did Sean placate his nephew? As Ryan rubbed the goose egg on the back of his head, he didn't feel sure about that. Sol dragged Patrick into the office and its holding cell, Sean following to see about bail. That left Mina and Ryan standing outside staring at the breath coming out of their mouths in place of a conversation.

"You can press charges," she said after a long pause.

His hand formed a fist to stop the incessant shaking. "You think I should?"

"I don't know. I don't know much anymore."

Ryan appreciated he wasn't the only one. "Oh, I forgot the reason I came here."

A few minutes later they stood with the sheriff, looking over the mold of the footprint. Sean had gone home, thinking it would be wise to let Patrick stew for a night.

"It's a fake Bigfoot," Ryan said as Mina hunched over it, examining its contours.

"Never thought it was Bigfoot," Sol said.

"No, I mean somebody carved a fake foot out of wood, hauled it up there, and left a few indentations in the snow. That's intent; that means—"

"Somebody killed Phil, and it wasn't an animal." Sol finished.

"And they did a pretty poor job of it." Ryan looked to Sol, who took Mina's place beside the foot. "Did you give it much of a look over?"

"No, I was focused on the human side of things." Sol pulled out his glasses and squinted for a better look. He rubbed his finger around the toes. "You can see the edge of the wood here. They didn't even bother to smooth the curves."

"But why do it at both scenes?" Mina asked. "It's not like we'd give up investigating and rule it a Bigfoot attack."

"Have you talked with Lane Jenkins? He's got a million-dollar TV deal if he can show proof of Bigfoot." Ryan pictured his friend lying in a tent with his insides spilled open and wondered what price that would bring in.

"It's not the same print as the first one." Sol straightened up.

Mina and Ryan turned to him. "How do you know?" she asked.

"Because that print I did examine at every angle and for several hours." He walked back to their evidence drawers and pulled out a similar mold.

Ryan pulled a small magnifying lens from his pocket. "You're right." Mina crept close to him, trying to see what he saw. He moved back so she could peer through. "Here, you can see the contours of the foot, the distribution of the weight."

"If it was the same person," she said, "wouldn't they get better with time, not worse?"

"Yes," Sol said. "It's possible the second capitalized on the first." He turned to Ryan. "Did you discover anything else up there?"

Ryan slapped his forehead. "The camera."

"What camera?" Mina and Sol said in unison.

Ryan pulled it out, and Mina grabbed a computer with an SD card portal. As soon as they plugged in the card, a folder opened with several photographs, timestamped.

"The camera is motion-sensitive. Once movement triggers it, it takes a series of photos."

Mina double-clicked on the first bunch of photos with a timestamp of 11 pm, all taken within a few minutes. Lane had placed the camera high in the tree, but with all the tall bushes surrounding it, it didn't shoot a lot of distance.

She clicked through the photos until the edge of a face popped into view.

"Dane," Ryan said. "Probably peeing. Sorry," he said with a glance toward Mina.

"Women pee too." She rolled her eyes.

"Yeah, I just mean...let's look at the next bunch."

"Why would he set up the camera where you guys designated a bathroom?"

"Bigfoot can be a territorial animal. The scent could draw him in. That's why we asked everyone to take their business outside the camp a bit."

"Let's open the next bunch." Sol interrupted.

The next series showed a rodent, probably a squirrel, climbing up a branch. Its eyes glowed in the infrared light. They went through each series, finding nothing more interesting than a rodent until a burst of images from 4:10 am.

The first image popped up on the computer screen, a hint of an ear on one side. The second one, barely more of a face but by the fifth, they could make out Phil's features.

"Do you think he was using the bathroom?" Mina asked.

"No," Sol said. "He's looking up, not down." They clicked on the next in the series.

"He's right," Ryan said. "He's looking for the camera. Lane had it fairly camouflaged in the branches." Sure enough a few photos later, Phil's arm was extending to their viewpoint.

The last of the photos opened. Phil had turned his head to face something behind him. His hand no longer reached for the camera.

Chapter 40

They went through the photos, several times, but they never saw what had caught Phil's attention in the moments before he died.

Mina could feel frustration radiating off Ryan. "Something lured him out of the tent," Ryan said. "He wouldn't have checked the camera in the middle of the night otherwise."

After going through all the photos again, Mina offered to drive Ryan back to Phil's cabin. Barely evening and already the stars filled the night sky over the highway. Another time, she would've pulled over to appreciate them.

"Mina," Ryan said as she killed the ignition and the silence rolled through the Jeep with the cold. "I don't know if Patrick did it or not or Lane, but there's something I should tell you. Sean and Dane were talking that night at camp about Patrick being in love."

She laughed. "Patrick falls for a new woman every month. Don't know if I'd call it love."

"That's why Dane found it odd. Said he'd finally fallen hard, and the girl had broken his heart the week or so before."

"No, he's not the...." She thought about the way he'd been acting since the season started, avoiding her, then apologizing to her. Adrienne had mentioned Patrick had been living with someone but had broken up. "Did they say who?"

"They speculated it might be you because you'd come to some family thing." Ryan caught her eye. "But they figured you were too smart to fall for him" His eyes widened as he waited for confirmation of her intelligence.

"I didn't break Patrick's heart." She pulled into the driveway of the cabin.

"Did he break yours?"

She scoffed. "Oh Ryan, getting hurt requires taking a risk. I don't take risks."

"Really?" His tone of voice called out her obvious lie.

"At least not on guys…at least on most guys." Why had she added that last part? Her face flushed, and she was very grateful the Jeep's dome light hadn't come on when she parked.

"What if he was in love with you?"

"What if he was; what's that got to do with anything?"

"Maybe he was jealous."

"Of Phil? That makes no sense."

"No, of me." She could feel his own flush come on, and she wondered how invisible she had been. "It's just, from the moment I met him, he didn't like me. Seemed really irked when I mentioned having lunch with you."

She turned off the engine, and the heat disappeared. "And what? He killed Phil thinking he was you?"

"You're right; it's a dumb thought."

"Yeah, nobody is going to kill someone over me." She'd once had two guys fight over her. But they were literally fighting across the table she'd sat at in the bar. The fight had been about another girl.

Knowing this conversation wasn't going anywhere beneficial for the pair of them, she had to end it. "I should go."

He leaned back in his seat and took a deep breath. "You're right; I'm sorry."

Part of her wanted him to press things, but a bigger part of her liked that she didn't have to argue the point.

He opened the door, heralding in a much-needed rush of cold air. "Goodnight, careful driving home."

She gripped the steering wheel and only nodded back as he walked inside. Mina was about 90 percent sure Patrick wasn't in love with her. However, she was 100 percent sure she didn't have feelings for him.

As she pulled out onto the dark road, a thought came to her so fast she slammed on the brakes. "No," she said out loud. "Patrick wouldn't."

Chapter 41

Mina sat beside Patrick on a small cot in the windowless room they called a cell, his usual cocky grin wiped away. "How long were you and Cate dating?"

His eyes slowly met Mina's. "This just between us?"

"I don't know if I can promise that."

"I just don't want to mess up her life."

"Holy cow, you are in love." She almost laughed, but the circumstances stopped that outburst. "So how long?"

"We started at the end of summer. I lost my housing around Thanksgiving and stayed with her for a few weeks." He gripped the edge of the cot. "But I never was around her kids. She's a good mom."

"How'd you manage that?"

"I wouldn't come in until they were asleep and left pretty early."

Sol sat just outside the door listening in. They both figured Patrick would be more apt to talk to her. "It ended when her husband came back?" Mina asked.

"It didn't exactly end."

"Oh, Patrick. You know better than that."

"It's not what you think." He stood up and paced. "They're separated and getting a divorce. Then he shows up at the beginning of December and wants to work things out. They hadn't told the kids yet, and she didn't want to toss him out before Christmas." He turned to Mina with a pleading expression. "After Christmas, they'll announce it and we'll be able to be together."

Mina had heard similar desperate words from other heartbroken friends over the years but Patrick? She wouldn't have believed him capable of that emotion. "Does James know?"

"I don't think so, but he can't find out. Mina, Cate says he's got a temper and can be controlling. Part of the reason she moved here was to get away from him. She figured with his work, this was the last place he'd want to live."

"Patrick, did you kill Phil?"

"Why would I?" he said. "What's that got to do with any of this?"

"Phil and Cate met for dinner. Maybe you thought he was competition."

"That's insane," Patrick exploded, making Mina inch away from him. "Cate just went out with him to organize some sort of gathering for those morons. No way she was interested in that dude."

Mina stood, not surer of his innocence than she had been ten minutes ago. The man proved capable of a lot deeper feelings than she gave him credit for. Sol followed her back into the office after she closed and locked the cell behind her.

"How did you know about the relationship?" Sol asked.

"His old winter boots were in Cate's hall closet." She explained about his need to buy new boots every season.

"Hold up." Sol went to the wall where they'd pinned several photos from the crime scene. After scanning all of them, and apparently not finding what he looked for, he went back to his office. Before she could ask what was going on, he returned with a stack of printed photos.

She looked over his shoulder as he spread them out on their conference table. "I didn't much look at the footprints around the campsite; I only focused on the crime scene.

"There," he said, pointing at a shot of tracks going in and out of the tent. "I did spend a lot of time here, though, trying to understand how Phil made it back to the tent."

"Okay." She didn't see what had struck him.

"Those are Patrick's tracks. Everyone said he went in to apply first aid." He grabbed a photo with the footprints in blood. "These are the same tread. It's hard to tell from a photo, but I swear the tracks by the tent and the tracks where Phil was attacked are from two different people."

Mina stared at the photo. "How do you know?" She didn't ask out of doubt—nobody doubted Sol's tracking skills—but she wanted to learn.

"The weights in the snow were different. The original tracks pressed more deeply into the snow and on the heel. And it's hard to be sure, but the tread might be worn differently. We need those boots," Sol said.

"I know where they are."

* * *

Sol put in a call to the county attorney to get a warrant for the boots. She promised to call back in a hurry, which going by bureaucracy and their remoteness to anything resembling a judge, could be an hour or a few days.

"So, who wore the boots?" Mina asked. "You've got the Orricks, Lane, and Ryan." She flinched a little when she said Ryan's name. Hoping Sol didn't notice her stumble, she continued. "You think one of them brought the boots up to deliberately frame Patrick? Why not steal his boots from the tent?"

Sol went through his office door, before sitting at his desk and turning on his computer. Mina followed Sol, who closed the door behind her. "We also need to consider Cate and James Ellis."

"Sean doesn't think anyone is capable of finding their way up that trail outside of family."

"Thinking isn't knowing." Sol, who thought better with a map, pulled out the forest service map and spread it out. "The camp was far enough away from the snowmobiles, no one would've heard anything, and it was a full moon."

Mina really wanted to believe that option—however unlikely it seemed. "Maybe."

"Or, and more likely, the murderer was someone in camp with access to the Ellis's home."

Mina didn't want to say it, didn't want to believe it. "Ryan..." She swallowed and started again. "Cate invited Ryan over for dinner. I don't know for sure if he went." Not wanting a response, she plunged forward.

"But she could've reached out to Lane about hosting some sort of gathering. We can ask her."

Sol leaned back in his chair. "I don't want to tip them off until we have the warrant for the boots. Everyone with access is still a suspect. Keep digging into Phil. We need to know who had motive and if they had access."

Mina returned to her desk and forced herself to think about anything but Ryan, which meant she spent way too much time thinking about Ryan. Two men she'd dated were both suspected of murder; it was time to take a break from the little dating she did.

Maybe it was exhaustion from reading the same story of Phil's rise to success again and again but when she opened up the last link, she ignored the story and looked at the headline. Below that was the byline, and everything changed. They finally had a connection.

The reporter's name was Grayson Moore.

Chapter 42

Ryan, who traded on awkwardness, tried desperately to find something to say to the girl who sat in the passenger seat of Phil's Range Rover. What words are there for someone who has had both parents die?

Natalie had no way to get to her father's house, and Ryan had no way to pick her up. He apologized three times for driving Phil's car, promising it would be hers. She didn't really care, she said, one way or the other. Now they rode in silence.

He had nothing to offer her about the death other than what he'd first told her. Her brother had canceled his flight, not ready yet to deal.

"Are you staying here?" she asked as they pulled into the driveway of a cozy cabin that belonged in a postcard. "No, I'm at the hotel." He'd already packed his stuff, not wanting to be in her way.

He helped her carry her bags into the house where they both stood uncertainly. "He's really gone, isn't he?" she said in a voice far younger than her twenty years.

Ryan so desperately wanted there to be another answer to that question. "He talked about you and your brother all the time."

She turned away from Ryan to stare at the window facing the jagged peaks of the Lost Gorge mountains. "He wanted us to come for Christmas, but we both have retail jobs and couldn't leave."

"He said he was proud of you two for making your own way."

She turned around. "Did he tell you it was his idea? He'd pay for our tuition, he said, but everything else was up to us." She spoke without anger.

"It was okay, though. For a long time, he was just a paper millionaire. It wasn't until he sold the company the real money came in, and by that time we were grown."

Ryan longed for a word, any word, that could make this bearable for her. "He told me once he regretted all the work he did when you were young. Said, at that time, he thought his payday was just around the corner. Then he went around the corner and you were grown and your mom was gone."

Natalie flinched when he mentioned her mother. "Then he up and decided to chase fake monsters in the woods with you." Now the bitterness came in.

Ryan decided he'd better go before he said anything else to cause pain.

He'd set his stuff in the back of the Range Rover in case Natalie could drop him off at the hotel, but he didn't want to bother her. As he pulled his bags out of the back, he noticed a small box marked "Sasquatch Research." Figuring that would upset Natalie more, he grabbed it along with his stuff.

Ryan needed a ride and wouldn't ask Natalie, didn't dare ask Mina, and figured Uber didn't operate here. He only knew one other person to call, James.

* * *

It wasn't James who pulled up; it was his wife, Cate.

Ryan sat in the passenger seat, having offered his thanks without knowing what else to say. In situations like this, he defaulted to saying nothing. His bag went in the backseat, but the box perched on his lap. He was curious to know what Phil had gathered about Bigfoot he hadn't shared with Ryan.

Cate pulled out onto the highway. "James has been wanting you and Mina to come over for dinner one of these nights. How long are you planning to stay in town?"

"I don't know. I was only due to come for a week but with everything that's gone on, I want to stay longer." He popped open the top of the box and it wasn't the Bigfoot stuff he'd been expecting. Instead, a bunch of financial papers and folders filled the box.

Ryan pulled out a stack to see if anything was underneath.

"What's that?" Cate asked with forced brightness. He took the hint she didn't want to talk about a death.

"Some of my friend's financial files I grabbed by mistake. I'll have to run it back to his daughter tomorrow."

Cate signaled as she slowed for a gas station. "Sorry, I want to fill up while I have the chance. My house is in the boonies." She pushed open her door. "Let me throw your stuff in the backseat."

Before he could protest, she'd come around and grabbed the box and threw it in the cargo hold.

Blessed silence filled the rest of the way to the hotel. "I'm sorry about your friend," Cate offered as they pulled into the parking lot.

Ryan mumbled something along the lines of, "Thanks, I mean I guess." He jumped out of the car and grabbed his gear from the back. He was pulling open the doors of the hotel before he remembered the box in the backseat.

He'd never acquired Cate's cell but sent a quick text to James. Hopefully, they could run it back before Cate got too far. He wanted to return the files as quickly as possible. If Phil had set it out, it might be important.

With his phone still out and in curiosity, he punched in the name of the company he'd spotted on the financial papers, HealthE Solutions. Without realizing it, he'd searched in image mode and the first images that popped up were mostly of James and one of Cate.

His finger hovered over the image in confusion and shock. He clicked on the image of Cate. It opened an article about "Catherine Orrick Hardaway, the woman behind the man."

Ryan stopped in the lobby, staring at his phone, oblivious to the clerk asking him for a reservation. None of this made sense. He thought their last name was Hanson. He also didn't know Cate was an Orrick, but considering how many Orricks he'd met in the last week it shouldn't be that much of a surprise. Why had she lied about her name?

Why did Phil have a box filled with papers about a company James and Cate owned? Phil had been a brilliant financier. Had James requested help with something? Ryan didn't know what was in that box or who it belonged to, but he didn't want to lose something of Phil's.

180

He would pick it up that day.

Mina's number went to voicemail. He punched the number of Sean Orrick.

Chapter 43

With a message to Grayson's sister to call her back immediately, Mina and Sol turned their attention to Patrick.

Mina sat across from her former friend, taking note of his black eye and wondering which fist had met a target. "I noticed your old boots in Cate's coat closet. It's how we knew about the affair."

"I'm not talking about Cate."

"We're not here about Cate," Sol said. "We're here about the boots."

"Why?" Before either could respond understanding creased his face. "You think someone else wore them to kill Phil. I knew you didn't think I could do it." He jumped to his feet and punched the air in front of him before enveloping Mina in a hug.

Mina gasped, and he returned her to her feet. "We're still investigating."

He ignored that. "If you think they were used in the murder, why would Cate have them?" The jubilant of the moment left him. "James?"

"Why would James kill Phil?"

"Because he's violent; maybe he thought she was with Phil. Is she safe, the kids?" He slammed his hand against the desk. "Of course, she's not. She's been trying to get away from him for a year."

"Did she tell you he hurt her?" Mina now understood better the argument she'd overheard.

"No, not in so many words, but I could tell she was nervous about him. Said she wanted to be a thousand miles away when he got the divorce papers. Maybe that's what brought him back."

"Can you call her about getting your boots back?" If Patrick picked them up, it would save a warrant. "But be chill about it," Mina said, "like it's not a big deal. We don't want her to inadvertently tip James off."

Cate's voice came through the phone with a softness Mina had never heard in the woman's tone as she answered Patrick's call. "Are you okay? I heard you were arrested."

"I'm okay. I freaked out on the guy who I thought killed Phil."

"They have someone? Who is it?"

"He's nobody just someone who was up at the camp with us." He explained about his boots getting taken by the police. "I can't find my old pair, and I think I left them there."

"I don't think I've seen them," she said with some hesitation. "But I'll look."

* * *

Grayson's sister returned Mina's call and wasted no time with a greeting. "Have you heard anything about Gray?"

"No, sorry. I take it he still hasn't been in touch."

"No." Her pain stretched all the way from New York. "He hasn't called the kids to wish them a Merry Christmas, not even a gift. He hasn't forgotten once since they were born."

"I'm curious about his career. You said he used to work on financial articles a few years ago. Why did he stop?"

"He's been floundering a bit, after his divorce, trying to find his next path. Got tired of doing a bunch of stories about rich people or people willing to do anything to get rich. That's why he started doing the outdoors stuff, but that was just a Band-Aid."

That truth cut a little too close to Mina. "Are you familiar with some of the articles he wrote?"

"I always tried to read them, especially the exposés."

"Exposés?"

"Yeah, his articles actually kicked off investigations that put people in jail."

Everything Mina had read about Phil had been positive, even the article by Grayson. "Can I email you a couple of photos and see if you recognize anyone from his stories?"

"Sure."

Not ten minutes after Mina sent a few images of everyone who was at the campsite and Cate and James, her phone buzzed with a text. *I don't know about most of them; I'll keep looking. But the other guy I recognized immediately. Here's a link to the latest article.*

Mina clicked on the link, expecting to see the same article on Phil. The headline that filled her screen caused her to gasp. "Sol," she yelled out. "You need to see this."

SEATTLE START-UP FOUNDER IMPRISONED FOR BILKING BILLIONS

Mina scrolled through the article on her phone while Sol brought up the link on his computer.

The first paragraph read:

Seattle start-up founder Jim Hardaway was sentenced to five to eight years on Thursday...

Mina scrolled back to the top looking for a date. Three years ago in January; James should still have been in prison. "Did he escape?"

Sol pulled up his computer with Mina hovering behind him. "Judge granted him a new trial and released him on bail a few weeks ago. Maybe he goes after the reporter for revenge."

"He didn't drive up until the week after Grayson died." Mina argued.

"That's what he told you. But he was released a full four days before the first attack. No telling how long he'd been here."

"What do you want me to do?"

"Get a hold of the prosecuting attorney and find out if either Grayson or Phillip were part of the original trial," Sol said. "I'm going to see about getting a warrant for his arrest. I doubt the conditions of his bail allowed him to leave the state. I want him in jail tonight."

Chapter 44

Ryan jumped in Sean's pick-up before it came to a complete stop. "Thanks, I appreciate the ride." He'd explained the situation.

"You think I'm related to this Cate person?" Sean asked.

"Her maiden name is Orrick."

"A lot of Orricks in this world, but if she's in this town, we are probably family. Although, the name doesn't ring a bell, and I don't recall anyone moving back lately. That would've meant a barbecue at the very least."

"What's with the snowmobile?" Ryan gestured to the sled propped in the truck bed.

"Checking some fence lines this week. It's easier to keep it loaded."

They passed the road marked with a street sign matching the address Cate had given him when she mentioned having him over for dinner. "That was it," Ryan said.

Sean pulled off onto the shoulder to turn around when an SUV pulled out, carrying James. The same SUV where Ryan had left the box.

"There he is. Can we follow him?"

Sean shot him a cross look. "Why don't you just call him?"

"I did. No one answered." Ryan pressed on at Sean's incredulous look. "Listen, I stole that box out of Phil's house, and I need to return it. It belongs to his daughter, and she should decide what to do with it."

Sean wrenched the stick into first gear and pulled out. "What's your plan? He's not heading toward town."

Ryan usually had a plan but hadn't since Mina crashed into his car. "If he stops someplace public, I'll act like we ran into him and ask about the box."

"And if he doesn't?"

"Let's just see where he goes."

Where he went was miles down the highway before pulling off to head down a snow-packed side road.

Sean pulled off again.

"I know," Ryan said. "We can't follow him down."

"Yes, we can," Sean said. "That's my family's private property. I'm responsible for it, and I keep track of who's going up there. And nobody is supposed to be up there."

"Where does it lead?"

"Our hundred-year-old cabin that can only be accessed by snowmobiles, which he doesn't seem to have. You can go a few miles until a canyon where you have to stop and sled in. I'm following him." Sean engaged his four-wheel drive. "You in or you out?"

"I'm in." They pulled off the black pavement onto a snow road.

Chapter 45

Mina read through all the articles about James Hardaway, starting with the latest.

The technology James had invented was supposed to change the world. Anyone with a smartphone would be able to check their temperature, blood pressure, cholesterol, and a host of other things. Your phone would send an alert to you and your doctor at any alarming change. There'd be no waiting for the chest pains to tell you were about to die from a heart attack.

He would've revolutionized healthcare, if only it had worked.

Instead, the entire company and its world-changing technology were nothing more than mirrors reflecting what others had already done. Mina found Facebook pages filled with angry investors, wanting their money back—desperate for their money back.

Modest estimates of the capital raised started in the $500 million with some believing at least a billion had been raised. When she read that, Mina leaned back in her chair trying and failing to grasp that kind of amount.

At least half a billion. Supposedly raised to fund research, development, overhead, and a whole lot of expenses a new company requires. The question became whether James had set out to build a product or fund a shell company.

When a company fails, investors lose their money. But did these investors lose their money to bad luck or a dishonest founder? The early articles at first questioned the promises of James, then they questioned James himself. One reporter visited the company's headquarters, incognito, and reported one floor had been done up with offices, meeting rooms, and a flurry of employees typing on computers and writing on whiteboards. He'd slipped away from the tour to discover the rest of the building was floors filled with empty cubicles.

His teams of lawyers would argue bad luck and bad press had led to the company's downfall. Eventually, an investigation would reveal James had been a glorified snake oil salesman.

The arrest warrant of James Hardaway arrived in Lost Gorge. Mina sat on hold with the FBI, trying to reach their contact about Phil's murder. They'd officially crossed the line into stuff the Feds care about.

Sol buttoned his coat. "I'm not waiting for someone else to die or for him to realize we're on to him."

Mina grabbed her own coat, but Sol stopped her. "I need you to stay here and make contact with an agent. Plus, you don't have the training yet to make an arrest."

"You're not going by yourself?"

"Nope, I'll pick up Clint on the way out."

The wind slammed the door shut as he left. Not long after, the phone rang with a Seattle area code. The district attorney prosecuting the case against James had finally returned her calls.

"You have James in custody?" The strident voice belonging to a woman named Anne didn't allow for any excuses.

"The sheriff has gone to arrest him, barring any problems."

"There shouldn't be. Each time we brought him in, he came peaceably, albeit with a team of lawyers. I am surprised he left the state, though. He didn't strike me as a runner, and the most jail time he's facing is five years if we can get another conviction. Not worth being a fugitive for."

"You said if. You think there's a chance he's innocent."

Anne laughed. "No, that man is as guilty as Cain, but he has very good lawyers. And the penalties for financial crimes aren't as strict as they should be. A lot of these guys see a few years in a white-color jail as a small risk for a big reward."

Mina stared at her computer and the article she'd been reading about James and Cate's great gift to charity. It had been written pre-arrest and featured the handsome couple in formal wear and holding glasses of champagne. "Do the names Phillip Griffith or Grayson Moore mean anything to you?"

"Phillip maybe sounds familiar, but I know Grayson was one of the reporters covering the first trial. He'd call me now and then for a quote."

"Was he a big part of the investigation or a source?"

"Oh no, it was another reporter who first broke the story and brought it to the authorities' attention. Grayson came in on it late."

Mina explained about the two deaths. "You don't think killing him would change the outcome of the second trial?"

"No, he's not a witness or a part of it. James is the kind of guy who's always one step removed from the dirt. It's why we've had a hard time getting charges to stick. I am sorry to hear about Grayson, though. He said he wanted to take the story in a new way."

"What do you know about James's wife?"

"Loyal, that woman is not. As soon as we arrested James, she took off. Most women do the whole 'Stand By Your Man' thing, at least until the guy goes to prison. She's smarter than average."

Cate was much smarter than average. "What about the money? Who ended up with that?"

"We put a freeze on all accounts and passports as soon as the investigation started. They lived fairly high on the hog with a mansion, private jets, and keeping up the appearances of a functioning company. The money was accounted for, if all spent. And a lot of the fortune was in paper money, stocks. Once the company went belly up, that vanished."

"None of this makes sense," Mina said more to herself than the attorney.

Typing came from the other end of the phone. "Hey, I figured out where I heard the other guy's name, Phillip. He was a partner in an equity firm that was one of the earliest investors. They lost millions, as in hundreds of."

"But he was one of many?"

"Yep, we've identified about a hundred different investors."

Mina hung up the phone more perplexed than before. James had no reason to murder Grayson, while Phil had more reason to murder him.

Why had Cate run away? To get away from James, from the scandal? Up until a few weeks ago, he'd been in jail.

Not twenty minutes after Sol left, he called. "Call in the state police, get all the deputies, and meet us at the trailhead where Phil was murdered."

Mina grabbed a jacket and her police belt. "What happened?"

"James took the twins into the mountains. Cate says she told him to move out, and he flipped out."

"Where are you going?" She slipped on her belt. The weight of the gun and taser tugged on her pants.

"We found his truck at the trailhead." Clint and I will start making our way up. You get everyone there."

"Is Cate with you?"

"No, she's—" The phone cut out.

"Sol."

Mina called in every reinforcement she could think of and ran out the door for her Jeep.

Chapter 46

The snow blew across the highway as Mina drove to the trailhead. By the time she'd make her way back, there would be foot-deep drifts to push through. If and when they made their way back. Her phone buzzed, and Cate's name flashed on the screen.

"Are you okay?" Mina asked by way of greeting.

"Mina," Cate shouted out of the phone as if walking through a wind tunnel, which considering the weather wasn't too far off the mark.

"James just called me." Wherever she was, the background noise softened and so did her voice. "He's got the kids. He said it was time we became a family again, and he wants me to meet him." Her voice broke at the end.

"Are the kids okay? Sol said—"

"James said they're fine, but ever since he came home…"

"We know about his sentence, Cate. The FBI is on its way. Where are you supposed to meet him?"

"He said he wouldn't go back to prison," the broken woman said.

"You need to tell me where you're meeting him."

"He just texted me directions to some cabin. If he sees me come up with anyone, I'm afraid of what he'll do." A sob broke out. "I thought coming here would be a fresh start. We could put the past behind us." Her voice grew strong. "I'm going to meet him; I have to believe he won't hurt us. I just needed to tell you in case, in case….Goodbye, Mina." The call ended.

Mina stared at the phone and her last connection to Cate. Tracing the location wouldn't do a bit of good. It would take too long and, in the end, would only ping off the one tower servicing Lost Gorge.

Sol had said James took the kids into the mountains. Now Cate was saying they went to some cabin. Mina pulled off the road and into a drift; her calls to Sol went unsurprisingly unanswered. She sent a text to his GPS, which may or may not go through.

Where was the family?

Why had Cate not given her the information? Cate was smarter than that. Mina didn't understand how she could be so… She wouldn't be. She said every situation could be turned to her advantage. How was this to Cate's advantage?

The prosecuting attorney had mentioned Grayson wanted to take a new angle on the story. What if that new angle was Cate?

Mina pulled out her phone and called Grayson's sister. Grayson's laptop, she said, had disappeared with him, but he'd gifted his old one to his niece for school. "He cleaned off the hard drive before he gave it to her. You won't find anything on it."

"How did he back up his files? To the cloud?"

"I don't know."

"Can you look for some icons like—"

"Wait, I found something." Mina held her breath as she waited for the answer. "It looks like a ton of work stuff."

"Send over anything with the Hardaman or the HealthE Solutions name."

Mina sat on the side of the road in a Jeep no longer warm sorting through files on her iPad. To anyone else the terms and numbers wouldn't make a whole lot of sense. To Mina, who'd interned her senior year in the law department of Goldman Sachs, they came through as clear as the sky after a blizzard.

Not all of the money had been accounted for.

James and Cate had a whole lot of reasons to want Grayson Moore dead—25 million of them. She also had a maiden name she hadn't told anyone in town. With that Mina had an idea of where Cate was headed.

That never-earned law degree was finally paying off.

192

Chapter 47

The SUV sat parked at the base of a small canyon only wide enough for a single-lane road now covered in snow. As Sean pulled off to the side, Ryan jumped out and looked through the back window of the SUV next to them. They'd taken the box out. Another SUV with an empty trailer was parked next to it.

Phil stomped around the truck. "The cabin is another mile in. I'm going to take the snowmobile up and figure out what's going on."

"What's your big worry?" Ryan's need to get the box back receded with each mile they followed a family taking a long weekend.

"We've had people breaking in and damaging the place. Then last summer, someone who got a key from someone came up to stay at the same time a family member came up. It turned into a brawl. I'm responsible for it; technically my immediate family owns the deed."

Sean dropped the tailgate to unload the snowmobile. "My grandfather built it during World War II, sure that the Japanese were on their way. He made it to be sturdy and hidden. We keep it stocked with firewood. A wood stove heats the place, and a generator runs the lights." Ryan helped Sean place the ramp on the tailgate.

"You can wait here. I won't be more than an hour," Sean said.

"No, I'll come with." Ryan was curious to know why Phil had those documents.

They sped up the canyon with walls so high light would only reach its floor at noon. They parked at a small tin shed; its front doors open revealing a snowmobile parked inside. The canyon opened up into a meadow surrounded by thick trees.

"Wait here. The house is about 100 yards up." Sean said as he jumped off the machine. "I'm going to knock on the door and see what's up."

Ryan acquiesced, not wanting to get in the middle of a private family situation. He'd have time to ask his questions after Sean settled things out. He waited on the leather seat of the snowmobile, the engine block keeping him warm.

How much time had passed since Sean left, ten minutes, twenty? He checked his phone for the time, but it had shut off in the bitter cold. The wind blowing through the canyon muffled any sound from the road. Though still technically daylight, the canyon's shadows grew long and dark.

The engine grew cold and so did he.

Ryan jumped off and stepped into Sean's tracks. He'd go up to the cabin and see what's going on.

Fifty feet up, a gunshot literally stopped him in his tracks.

Chapter 48

Mina tried again to reach Sol, but still no answer. She sped down the highway, leaving snow blowing across the pavement behind her. The turn off to the cabin was about a mile from the mouth of Lost Gorge canyon. She'd visited there once a few summers ago during one of the on portions of her relationship with Patrick.

Lights flashed on a warning sign on the highway. The high winds in the canyon were creating drifts, requiring vehicles to have four-wheel drive or chains. That would slow down any help that would be coming from the state and feds.

When they did arrive, all help would be going to the trailhead Sol had gone up. Before she diverted everyone, she needed to know for sure if Cate had gone to the Orrick cabin.

Fresh sets of tracks on the unpaved road signaled someone had driven down. Her Jeep plowed through the snow as she hit the gas. Two SUVs and a truck she recognized as belonging to one of the Orricks were parked at the mouth of the canyon. She jumped out to check the cars—empty. Snowmobile tracks showed where everyone had gone.

Mina carried a radio that reached no one at this distance. She would have to return to the highway to call in reinforcements.

As she climbed back into the Jeep, the sound of a shot echoed through the canyon and across the snow-covered flats.

She jumped in and gunned her engine and shot up the canyon. The kids were up there.

Chapter 49

As a scared teen, Ryan had run away without thinking from the danger. Now he ran without thinking again, following the road to the cabin. He abandoned the tracks and the snowmobile and dashed into the trees. He'd left the girl; he wouldn't leave Sean.

Thick bushes slowed him down, which was probably a good thing considering the noise he made busting through. He reached into his pocket and pulled out a headlamp he'd carried with him ever since his and Mina's long night. Only a hint of daylight lined the high canyon walls.

Not wanting to make a target out of his head, he turned the light on but kept it in his hand and pointed to the ground. He found his way through the few openings in the trees toward what he hoped was the cabin and Sean. After a while, he didn't need the headlamp as the soft lights of the cabin broke their way through the forest.

A large area around the cabin had been cleared of trees for about twenty yards, making it impossible to approach it without being seen. Ryan laid on his stomach and crept to the edge.

The windows were covered with drapes that let out light and nothing else. The hum of a generator powered the cabin.

Nothing moved and no sign of Sean.

Ryan didn't have a good decision to make. Taking the snowmobile to go get help would take hours, and he couldn't abandon Sean. But maybe he was a fool; Sean could be right now sitting in the house working things out or by the shed, wondering what happened to him.

Ignoring those thoughts, Ryan crept closer to the house. Even with all his layers, the cold forced its way through as he lay on the frozen ground. He clenched his jaw to gain control of his shaking teeth as he crawled his way around the edge of the woods to be closer to the front porch.

All of his creeping was for not as a gun cocked behind him.

Chapter 50

The sound of the gun cocking echoed through the trees. Mina's gun, an automatic, didn't require a bullet in the chamber, but she wanted to get this guy's attention without making too much noise. She also didn't want to speak and let him know she was a woman. Let whoever think she was a six-and-a-half-foot Marine.

She angled her headlamp directly on the man's face as he turned over. With his hands shading his eyes, she knew she wouldn't appear as anything more than a shadow.

"Don't shoot," the man said.

"Ryan?"

"Mina?"

She lowered the gun a few inches before lifting the gun back up. "What are you doing here?"

Ryan yanked his head to the cabin behind him. "Keep your voice down," he whispered. "Do you want them to hear you?"

"Who?" Her suspicion reared up at his constant ability to show up in the wrong place.

He hesitated. "I don't know. Whoever fired the shot."

"Show me your hands." She demanded.

He held them up, empty. Mina shone the light around the area. The blast she'd heard ricocheting through the canyon resembled a rifle, not a pistol. But she couldn't be sure; she'd been far away. She'd gotten her Jeep halfway up the canyon before the snow had sucked her in, and she had come the rest of the way on snowshoes.

"What are you doing out here?"

"I came with Sean. His family owns this house, and he found out Cate and James had come. Wanted to see what was what while I waited by the shed." Ryan scooted deeper into the forest and closer to her. His proximity didn't lessen her anxiety. She couldn't get a read on him and that drove her crazy. She needed a category to file him in. Suspect, date, crazy person, something.

"Then the gun went off," he continued. "I can't find Sean. I've been trying to get closer to the cabin to see what's up. Why are you here?"

"James has a warrant out for his arrest." She crouched down beside him with a view of the house.

"Why are you here alone? Where's the sheriff?"

"On his way." That could be a lie, but she hoped she told the truth. "You head back down the canyon road and wait for him. I'm going to get closer to the house and see what's going on."

"I'm not leaving, not until we find Sean."

Mina faced the cabin and the shadows that moved behind the curtains. She didn't have time to argue. "Ten minutes. Stay here, and I'll be able to find you." A large granite boulder, twice as tall as Mina sat in the middle of the woods, probably a piece broken from the canyon walls. "Then if I don't come back, you promise me you'll go down to the road and call out."

He reached out and took the sleeve of her coat. "You're not going alone."

"If something happens, one of us needs to get out and get help."

He thought of Sean and the gunshot. "Ten minutes."

Mina crept through the trees to the back of the house where the lights didn't shine.

On the other side of the cabin, the heavy brush grew closer to the porch. It would offer more concealment to creep to a window.

Mina's heavy breath crystallizing in the night air didn't come from exertion. She tried to calm her rapid heart, which seemed to pulsate through her entire body. Each side of the house offered no more information than the first. She came around the last corner to the front. Here the yard had been cleared from the road in.

Lights from the windows shone on the porch and cast shadows onto the white snow. Untracked snow covered the yard except for several sets of footprints coming from the road.

One window facing the porch wasn't covered with any drapes. Probably to look out and see if anyone was coming. Mina needed to get to that window without anyone seeing her. She would advance from the side where she had cover and come around the porch.

Her jacket and snow pants were completely black, which helped in the shadows but would call way too much attention when crossing snow.

She imagined a gun pointing out of every window, waiting for her to expose herself. Had Phil sense evil in the woods? Would she know what it felt like to lie in the snow as your life drained away? "Stop it," she whispered. "Do it now."

She ran across the snowy expanse and didn't stop until she flattened herself against the cabin. Even if they looked out the side windows now, they wouldn't see her.

How much time did she have before she was due to meet Ryan? She didn't want him doing something impulsive. Her watch glowed with the numbers, six more minutes. She made her way to the corner. One last turn and she'd be in the light. With her teeth, she ripped off her glove and slipped her gun out of its holster. The cold metal offered a small degree of reassurance.

She turned the corner and inched her way around to the porch, keeping her back to the wall. She slipped over the railing like she mounted a horse. Praying no one had come in the last minute to peer out, she crept to the window and looked in.

Cate, her back to Mina, stood in what appeared to be a living room with couches and a game table set up. She threw stuff from the table into a box propped on her hip, green and red plastic things.

Monopoly? They were playing Monopoly. Mina tried to smack her forehead with her hand before realizing she still carried a gun.

All of this and the family was taking a simple retreat? No, that didn't make sense. What about all the calls claiming James was going to hurt the children? Had that been a misunderstanding the family had sorted out? Where was Sean?

Before Mina could decide whether it might be a good idea to just knock on the door and say hello, Cate paused in her cleaning of the game. She straightened up and stared down at the box as if debating its contents.

She flung the box across the room, its pieces and money flying all over. With one swift swap, she knocked over the table sending the game board crashing to the ground. Mina tightened the grip she'd just relaxed.

Cate turned around. "Aren't you dead yet?

Chapter 51

Had Ryan dared to take a standing position, he would've been pacing the woods. Instead, he kept perfectly still while his blood did the rushing.

He didn't bother to check the time. Ten minutes or not, he wouldn't be leaving Sean and definitely not Mina to their own devices. A movement caught his eye; Mina came around the side of the porch to one of the front windows. After a second, she crept to the door.

It was like watching a horror film, and he wanted to scream out 'not to open that door.'

He moved to a crouching position like a sprinter waiting for the starting gun. Ryan could cover the ground in a few seconds should he need to; he'd ignored the pain from his feet this long. He inched forward to get as close as possible to Mina.

She retreated from the porch and faded back into the darkness. He didn't so much as sigh in relief. He didn't have the breath for it nor the inclination to make that much noise. *She probably saw Sean inside talking with the family. Everything is fine and you are both overreacting.*

He held onto that sentiment as long as he could, which was less than a minute. That's when he saw the slight movement in the front yard, a few feet beyond the forest's edge. A hand reached up out of the snow.

Chapter 52

Mina jumped back from the window, sure Cate stared straight at her. But, no, the other woman's attention seemed directed another way.

With an annoyed glance, Cate strode out of sight but returned carrying a knife. She made her way toward the door and disappeared from view.

A part of her Mina didn't know existed took over and instead of running back and out of sight, she crossed the five or so feet to the door determined to meet the fight head-on. She lifted her weapon and placed her finger on the trigger.

The door never opened.

She grabbed the doorknob and turned—locked. With one hand still holding up her gun, she lifted the other to pound on the door but thought better of it at the last second.

All Cate had to do was refuse to open the door, and there wouldn't be much Mina could do about it. While she would try to find a way in, Cate could continue whatever plan she had. Mina had read about too many family murder/suicides to believe she could stop this by talking. She also couldn't account for James. Was he part of this? Would Mina be taking on two armed killers?

Mina returned to the window but couldn't see Cate or the knife. She leaned forward trying to find an angle that would offer more visibility. On her tiptoes, she could barely make out the floor closest to the front of the house.

Was that blood? A dark stain soaked the braided rug by the door.

Could she break a window? These weren't cheap panes but thick ones to help hold out the cold. By the time she could crawl through Cate would be on her with the knife and whatever other weapon she carried.

Do something, her brain screamed.

There had to be something, a back door or an open window. She scooted backward away from the window. Her heel found the edge of the porch, and she slipped back into the blackness.

She would send Ryan for help while she tried to find a way in. The entire trip around the house lasted less than eight minutes. She returned to the large granite boulder.

Of course, Ryan was gone.

She whispered his name, once, then louder. A branch broke in the thick brush, and she fumbled for her gun, cursing that she'd put her glove back on. Before she could lift it up, Ryan whispered. "It's me. I found Sean."

* * *

Ryan had drug Sean through the snow and back into the trees where he lay gasping for breath.

Blood soaked into the wet snow from his thigh, taking Mina back to the day that started all this. She knelt next to him. "We'll get you out."

He sucked in air. "Shot me from the house when I was walking up. Didn't see who."

Cate had to be expecting the police to show up eventually. Maybe she or James mistook Sean for them. "Ryan is going to haul you to the snowmobile and get you out."

"No," Ryan whispered.

"We all leave together," Sean said.

"I can't leave without knowing the kids are safe." Mina had a hard time believing the woman who picked up the twins from ski school with a hug could hurt them. But the dead men in Cate's wake would argue differently. She would not underestimate this woman.

"I've got to get into the cabin," she said. "I've got to find the kids.

Sean sat up; his face creased with pain. "I know a way in."

Chapter 53

On the other side of the cabin, where the woods grew the thickest, a small trellis covered in vines wound its way to the upper windows. "We used to sneak out to howl at the moon when we were kids." Sean had told Mina when describing the spot.

She studied the trellis, weighing their very bad options. Ryan pulled at the wood, but she put a hand on his shoulder and shook her head. That thing wouldn't stand the weight of a normal man but maybe it could a small, okay, very small woman. Not to mention the tiny window in the loft it led to.

Mina found a foothold and pulled herself up. A few feet off the ground she hesitated, but the trellis held. Hand over hand she continued up until reaching the window. To her surprise, since nothing about the day had proved easy, the window slid up without trouble.

Nothing stirred in the room as it lay in complete darkness. The window was so small the only way through would be headfirst. Not exactly the best way to enter a room ready for a fight.

Under her feet, a piece of the old trellis snapped off. Before she could break it completely, she grabbed the windowsill for support and pulled herself through the open window. Halfway through, when her hips met the edge, she got stuck.

Downstairs it sounded like Cate was throwing things against a wall. Mina frantically undid the zipper of her snow pants and her utility belt. She pulled the belt through the window and dropped it on the floor. Like a snake shedding its skin, she pushed herself through.

She landed on a hardwood floor with a thud, her pants around her ankles.

The moving downstairs stopped and footsteps sounded. Mina slid the window closed, grateful it didn't squeak.

On the other side of the loft, a soft light shone from a staircase leading downstairs. The footsteps grew closer. Mina rolled away from the window behind something solid, a bed. Unfortunately, the bed came too close to the floor to enable her to crawl underneath.

The steps stopped just inside the loft. A light, maybe a lantern, highlighted the room casting odd-shaped shadows.

Mina reached down for her gun but only found emptiness. It and the belt still lay in a pile by the window. She grimaced as the light moved around the room. She was about to be caught, literally, with her pants around her ankles. With their synthetic material, pulling them up would be like sending off a flair to her position. But leaving them down would make it far harder to fight off an attack.

The light grew larger. Steps went to the side of the room across from her. The light must've come from a lantern as it gave off a more haloed effect versus direct. After a few seconds, the light grew closer. With her face pressed flat against a rug, she could make out a set of legs on the other side of the bed.

Mina lay flat and forced her body to stay entirely still. What she couldn't control, though, was the trembling of every inch of her. She pressed her lips closed to keep from screaming.

After an eternity, or only thirty seconds, the light receded. Footsteps retreated down the stairs.

She pulled her pants up as she stood. Someone lay in the bed, and Mina dropped down, waiting and listening? How had anyone slept through her crash through the window?

From the floor, she peered up over the bed into the face of Kelly fast asleep.

Before Mina could experience any relief, the complete stillness of the child set off alarms. Despite not knowing what she'd do if it worked, Mina reached out and grabbed Kelly's arm, shaking her slightly, then harder. Nothing.

She ripped back the covers laid her cheek against Kelly's lips. A small amount of breath came out. Alive. She shook off the tears of relief and used her fingers to sort out a weak pulse. *Please don't let me be too late.*

With one stride, she was across the room to the other bed. Mina found Chris in a similar state. She could only assume they'd been drugged. Enough dosage to keep them asleep or enough dosage to ensure they didn't wake up?

Either way, she had to get them out.

Downstairs the racket resumed. If James and Cate were down there fighting it out, she'd let them go at it.

Mina scooped the little girl into her arms, or tried to, the six-year-old was more than half her size and completely dead weight. Half-hunched over, she stumbled to the window and slid it up.

At the slight sound, Ryan looked up. She pushed the little girl's head partially out so he could see what she intended to do. His startled face in the moonlight turned quickly to steel, and he nodded. He would catch her, Mina knew this.

She wrapped her arms around the girl's chest and lifted her feet through the window. She wouldn't take a chance on sending her out headfirst. Kelly's head bobbed up and down, and she mumbled a "Mom." Mina wanted to rejoice at even that little bit of life but kept quiet.

Mina lowered her slowly out the window until she grasped Kelly by only the arms. "Okay," Ryan whispered from the bottom. Mina said a prayer that was no more than a whispered, "please." She let go.

The second she released her grip, she pushed her head through the window. Kelly laid across Ryan's shoulder, potato sack-style.

Mina did a quick fist punch in the air before turning back to Chris. As she reached his bed, more footsteps creaked on the stairs. She grabbed him and lunged to the window.

The steps reached their destination.

Chapter 54

As a child, Ryan had fallen in the cold waves of Ocean Beach in northern California. Each time he tried to find his feet another wave came and pummeled him into the sand. That same feeling of being pushed to the brink of death again and again had been his constant companion since getting off the plane.

He could've fled this place a week ago. But as Ryan trudged through knee-deep snow toward the woods, a little girl he barely knew over his shoulder, he held no regrets. He would save this girl.

Once he reached the woods, the snow thinned out and he moved as fast as the moonlight would allow. The girl slung over his shoulder didn't move but only offered the occasional groan. What had they done to her?

Once in the trees, he found a stump and propped her on it. She breathed, but barely. He grasped her shoulders and shook her slightly. She didn't respond. He did it again but harder, no response.

Glass broke in the cabin and he jerked around, but he couldn't see anything beyond the dim windows. He swallowed the yell on the tip of his tongue for Mina. He didn't know if she'd been discovered yet or not.

Behind him, the girl groaned. "Cold," she mumbled. Ryan ripped off his jacket, leaving him only a shirt, and bundled her up like a doll. He needed to run back to the cabin and find Mina. But what about the girl? He'd find Sean. Bullet hole or not, that man would protect her.

By the time Ryan made it to the spot where they'd left Sean, he was gone. Ryan swung around in a 360. This was the place; he could still spot blood on the smashed snow where Sean had laid.

The only other tracks led back to the mouth of the canyon. Ryan plunged ahead, doing a half leap through the deep snow.

Every attempt to run resulted in him tripping over a bush or a log and almost dropping the girl. He desperately wanted her to be able to wake up but didn't want it to be now. He could imagine the scream of a girl being carried out of her home by an almost stranger.

"Ryan."

He almost did drop the girl at the unexpected call of his name.

He whipped around to find Sean leaning on a stick for support. "I found their snowmobile key and figured we could use it to get everyone out or at least disable it so they can't follow." His eyes widened at the sight of the still girl in Ryan's arms. "Is she alive?" he asked with a hoarse whisper.

"Yes, but she's out of it. I've got to go back to Mina." He held out the girl as if making an offering. "Can you get her out on the snowmobile? We'll take the other one."

Sean weighed the options. "Get us to the sled. Once I'm on that, the leg won't matter."

They made it in an agonizing few minutes. It only took a few seconds to deposit the girl on the sled.

Sean stared at Ryan. "You two follow or I'm coming back for you."

Before Ryan considered his next step, a scream broke through the wind and dark.

Chapter 55

The light filled the room, ushering in Cate, knife in hand.

Mina clutched Chris to her, unsure whether holding him or putting him back on the bed was the right decision. Would his mother hurt him?

Then she saw the knife, more specifically the blood on the knife. Her gun lay behind her by the window still in its belt.

Whatever surprise Cate's face displayed at the sight of Mina, she quickly replaced it with relief. "Mina, you found us. Thank God."

"What's wrong with Chris?"

"James." Cate took a step forward without lowering the knife. "I think he gave the kids some Benadryl or something." Her eyes filled with tears. "He was going to kill us. He just tried to kill me downstairs. Mina, I…" Sobs burst from her as she held up the knife. "I think I killed him. He's downstairs on the floor. We need to get help."

Even at this moment, Mina couldn't help but be in awe of Cate's abilities. Despite everything she knew, everything she saw, she still wanted so much to believe this woman. Chris shifted in her arms, bringing her back to what was at stake in trusting her.

"Help is coming. Sol is bringing in the state troopers but let's get the kids out of here. I'll haul them out, okay?"

"Why isn't Sol or anyone else with you now?" All softness had bled out of her voice. "How long have you been here?"

A rush of thoughts crossed Cate's face as she calculated Mina's presence and what that meant. Mina could watch her life being measured and knew the end sum would be zero.

She shifted Chris from one arm to the other to conceal another step toward her gun.

Cate clenched the knife tighter, a decision made. "Put him down."

Mina still didn't know if the boy served as a shield or if his mother cared. Whatever he was, Mina wanted him out of the equation. The cold breeze carried from the window. If she pushed him through, how hurt would he be? And how quickly could she do it before Cate jumped her with that knife?

Mina took another step. "We know James just got out of prison, and we know he'll do anything to keep from going back. You did the right thing, the only thing to protect your kids. I'll tell them that when they get here. You didn't have a choice."

Cate smiled her oh-so-gregarious smile that could make a person feel right at home. "Oh Mina, you are a friend. Give Chris to me. I don't want him to be afraid when he wakes up."

The window was closer than the gun. Her arms ached at Chris's weight, and she would need to put him down soon. The snow creaked outside. A footstep? "Why did he drug them?" Mina couldn't fight as long as Chris was in the room.

Cate glanced at the other empty bed. "Probably didn't want him to know what was happening."

The girl's bed sat empty, but the bedding had been bunched up. Cate hadn't yet realized one twin was already gone.

They measured each other from across the room both knowing they lied to one another but neither yet ready to call the bluff. Did Cate hope what Mina did? That she'd be able to turn the tide in her favor before the moment when it all went down?

The window lay one more step away. Mina raised her voice in hopes Ryan waited below, ready to catch another kid. "Why don't I take the kids out of the house? Then we can sort this out."

Cate gestured to the staircase behind her. "Let's go." With each step Mina had retreated, Cate had taken two closer. Mina's heel scratched the wall behind her. It was now or never.

"I heard you before outside prowling around. Too bad I missed with the rifle."

Mina's backside touched the windowsill. She maneuvered until Chris's feet stuck out the window.

"You must've been around when I killed James." Her fake emotion disappeared as Cate had grown tired of the charade. "If you think holding onto Chris will save your life, then you're wrong."

Mina shifted him further out, but his clothes snagged on the sill. "You're not going to hurt your son."

"Grayson sure didn't think I'd hurt him when I jumped on the lift beside him at the last minute. You know, when I pushed him off over a ravine and then jumped after him when the ground was closer, he actually asked me to get help."

Mina fumbled for the snag, trying to unhook Chris. Cate advanced closer.

"He had no idea what I was capable of. I wonder if he figured it out before I stabbed him and left him to be covered by the storm. He bled out a lot." She shrugged as if knowing was nothing more than idle curiosity. "Whatever happened to him after I left, didn't do me any favors."

"What did happen?" Mina asked. Chris's pants tore out of the snag.

"I don't know, but you know, Mina, better than anyone what I'm capable of. I'm going to only ask once more. Put Chris down."

Before Mina could take a breath, Cate charged across the room. Mina shoved Chris as far as she could. He cried out.

Mina let go of his feet and brought her arm up to shield her face as Cate came at her with the blade.

Chapter 56

Mina dropped to the floor as Cate charged her and stabbed empty air. She jumped on Mina, who grabbed her arm in a desperate attempt to stop the incessant stabbing. Cate didn't aim; she kept stabbing until she could find a target.

The knife found a target. Mina yelled in pain as the blade sliced through her coat and into her forearm.

She thrust her hips in the air, sending Cate who straddled her onto the floor. Her belt and holster had disappeared into the shadows cast from the bed. Mina rolled to it, pushing the box spring up into Cate. Anything to create a barrier between her and the knife.

With the mattress between them, she charged Cate, slamming her into the wall.

Cate's grip remained tight on the knife, and she pushed right back. A slash through the thin mattress reached Mina's other side. She muffled her cry of pain, not wanting Cate to know she had an advantage.

A figure came up the stairs behind Cate, Ryan. He wrapped his long arms around her, pinning her arms to her side and pulling her away.

Mina dropped the mattress and rushed forward to grab her legs.

But Cate wouldn't be contained, and she wouldn't give up. She turned the knife on Ryan and stabbed him in his torso. His arms released, and he slumped to the floor.

She turned with her arm lifted. Mina jumped on the floor to find her gun.

Her mind didn't even register she had the pistol in her hand as she pointed it at Cate and fired and then again. Cate collapsed on the floor; she didn't even let go of the knife as the first bullet felled her.

She lay between Mina and Ryan, who stared at each other unable to believe they were still alive. Mina walked up to Cate who gasped for each breath. She grabbed the knife and wrenched it out of her still tight fingers. Cate glared at her with hatred, finally using an honest expression.

"Are you okay?" Ryan gasped.

"Yes. You?"

"The knife got tangled in my hoodie." He crawled to a standing position. "Mina, you are not okay."

Mina tore her eyes away from Cate and glanced down to realize she was bleeding through her jacket. "No, I'm not."

She sank to the floor. Ryan tore his hoodie off and pressed it against her side. Mina smiled weakly at him. "How many layers did you wear?"

He added more pressure, his eyes not meeting hers. "Didn't want to get cold again. I'll bring the snowmobile around and load you up."

Cate sputtered next to them. Ryan took the gun Mina had dropped next to her and pressed it back into Mina's hand. "I'll carry you downstairs," he said with his eyes on Cate.

"Just go get the sled. The closer, the better."

"I'll be right back." He jumped to his feet.

"The twins?" she whispered.

"Kelly is with Sean. I left Chris on the porch." Ryan jumped up and ran to the stairway, stopping once to look back at her.

Once he was gone, Mina scooted backward until she leaned against the open box spring. "Cate," she said as loud as the seeping blood would allow.

The body twitched. One hand opened and closed, and Mina wondered if she still was trying to grasp the now gone knife. Cate's mouth opened and blood trickled out.

Chapter 57

Mina opened her eyes to see Ryan sitting asleep in a chair beside her. She tried to lift a hand, but an IV with way too many drugs made the effort too much. The memories of the last few weeks, especially the last day, rushed in.

She examined this man whom she'd only known a short time and whose life had been decidedly traumatic since that day. His beard had filled in his gaunt cheeks, and his clothes showed the living they'd done. Mina smiled at a piece of duct tape across one knee.

The smile faded. Where were the twins? And where was Cate?

"Ryan."

He jumped to his feet, his eyes searching the room until he settled on hers. Mina attempted a smile. "Easy, buddy. It's not like I stabbed you."

"I'm sorry," he said. "Are you okay? I'll call the doctor."

She now knew what people meant when they described a stabbing pain. But if anyone ever used that phrase to mean a side ache, she'd smack them. "What happened with…" There were so many questions. "…with everything?"

"Let me get your doctor."

Before he could escape the room, she called out. "Are the kids all right?"

A sad smile crossed his face. "They're alive."

The doctor returned to tell her she was lucky to be alive, but she no longer had a spleen. She didn't feel as lucky then.

Sol hovered around the door until the doctor and Ryan left.

"Is Cate dead?" she asked as soon as they were alone.

"Yes, and James."

That settled in her gut with a different kind of hurt than the wound. She wanted so much for none of this to happen. "But the twins?"

"They're okay. Doctor said they'd been drugged, but not enough for permanent damage. You saved them."

She glanced out the window to view the white plains. The hospital they'd life-flighted her to had to be far away from the mountains of Lost Gorge. She'd remembered parts of the trip. A snowmobile ride and then a helicopter. "Did I? I still don't know if Cate would've hurt them."

Sol settled on her bed. "She killed her own husband. She may have killed at least two innocent men. You weren't in a position to know what she was fully capable of."

No, Mina could admit, she wasn't.

Chapter 58

The ski season ended in May, like it always did. The snow melted into an ugly muddy mess that finally yielded wildflowers, like it always did. But it seemed to take a long time that spring.

The same knife used to kill James and stab Mina had small traces of blood from Phil. They theorized Cate had killed both men and kept Patrick's boots to frame James.

The treasure trove of evidence on Grayson's computer gave Cate plenty of motive. She'd apparently taken money in the sum of $25 million under the table from less scrupulous investors than Phil. It had never been recorded and was never found.

Also found in Grayson's email was a message from Cate inviting him to town to do a story. He had no idea the woman he'd been investigating sat on the other side of the message.

Everyone had a guess about what happened to Grayson's body after Cate killed him. The popular theory was that wolves got to it. The other theory, one that would not go away, was that Bigfoot had torn it apart to haul it away.

Mina never said one way or another which theory she ascribed to. Better not to believe she knew everything, she decided. What mattered is that he went home to his sister to be properly mourned.

* * *

Mina waited on hold and had been for several minutes when a knock came at her door. Ryan didn't wait for her response and walked in. She mouthed 'just a second' as the receptionist came back to the line.

"We have you confirmed with a start date of June 1 for law enforcement training."

"Great, that's what I have," Mina said.

"Looking forward to it, Deputy."

She'd expected a huge objection from her mom when she'd explained her career choice. "I know this isn't what you wanted?"

"Is it what you want? Have you finally settled?" her mother had asked.

Mina had looked up to the high peaks surrounding the town she would serve. "Yes."

"Then be happy."

Mina hung up the phone as Ryan gave her a kiss. "Seriously eight weeks?" he said. "Don't they even have a spring break?"

"Oh, please. You won't even know I'm gone. You and Sean will be traipsing through the woods for Bigfoot mating season."

He shot her a stern look. "We men don't traipse," he said in a false bass before breaking a smile.

Saving the kids had released a lot of the guilt he'd carried. He now knew what sort of man he was. He still hunted Bigfoot, but more out of hobby than necessity. "Plus, I do have to get that website somewhat functioning."

"I know, so frustrating when work has to interfere with fun."

Ryan had moved to town full-time, working remotely as a freelance developer.

Though she'd finally accepted a full-time job with Sol, Mina insisted on one condition. She did not work on a powder day unless he'd already gone through every other deputy in a 100-mile radius.

Ryan had promised to learn to ski come winter.

An Excerpt from Killer in the Canyon

On the day an eight-year-old boy went missing in the mountains above Lost Gorge, the best man to find him was three hundred miles away fighting a forest fire.

Only a few threads of daylight remained by the time Sol Chapa, still reeking of smoke and sweat, arrived at the remote campsite. Making the last turn on the dirt road, his headlights swept from a wall of pines to glare on a hundred people standing around several bonfires. Despite the fun setting of a Fourth of July weekend, not a single person wore a smile and a few openly wept.

Sol, search and rescue commander, former sheriff, and current part-time deputy should've been first on the scene after the initial panicked call from the boy's parents. Instead, some idiot celebrating the holiday a week early had lit a mountain on fire. Sol, also a volunteer firefighter, had heeded the call.

The current Lost Gorge sheriff, Clint Gallagher, launched a search, but the first day had passed with no success, and then the second . . .

Sol parked his black van, which drove more like a tank with its large mud tires and high clearance, next to a thirty-foot motor home—search and rescue's mobile headquarters. Clint waited at the RV's doorway.

Sol took off his ever-present ball cap and ran his hand through thinning black hair that had been on its way out since high school but had accelerated the last few years. Hitting his forties and the death of his wife almost two years ago had aged him early. He killed the engine, the roaring diesel coming to a silence as he pushed the van door open. "You should've called me sooner."

"I thought we would find him the first day," Clint said. "Figured you were more needed at the fire."

"There are a few hundred people to fight fires but only me to search."

Clint stepped out of the doorway to allow his deputy to slide into the command center. "Last I checked, we have twenty well-trained volunteers."

"And yet here we are." The door slammed shut behind him.

Sol had personally trained each member of his team; he knew how good they were. But until he had a way to transfer his instinct into the trainees, he would forever be on call.

A family reunion had brought a few dozen families to the majestic, yet remote mountain site, which, due to its elevation, only stayed barren of snow a few months per year. Even in July, each summer storm carried the risk of snow.

The mountains around them stood in rugged defiance to the plains beyond. Their county lines bordered almost ten thousand square miles—bigger than some states. Plenty of folks tended to get lost or hurt, and search and rescue, or SAR, did its best to save each one.

With a cup of cold coffee and no intention of sleeping, Sol pored over the area maps.

The myriad of canyons above the campsite concealed a multitude of mines with more entrances than could ever be mapped. The county had done what it could with the popular spots and gated them off. Smaller holes, about the size of a boy, still dotted the cliffs but the closest had to be a few miles away.

Sol knew these mountains better than most people knew the path between their bed and bathroom, but the mines added a layer of complexity. His knowledge tended to the above ground. "Where have you searched so far?"

Clint sat across from him at the small pullout table. "The first night was spent canvassing the campground here and the lower sites as well. We went down a few trails but didn't want to risk destroying any track until we had daylight. The second day, we hit it hard, but the dogs couldn't get a good bead on his scent and every trail petered out. We've got more volunteers coming up tomorrow—at least a hundred."

"Show me the marked maps." The team would have meticulously marked each searched trail with a timestamp. There were no wasted efforts. Sol ran down each line, mentally removing them from his own plans. "What about the mines?"

"Every entrance we've found so far is still locked. I've sent for the state's experts, but they haven't arrived yet." Clint slumped in his seat. His freckles made him look younger than thirty-five, but the weight of the job had slowed his usual ready smile. He'd held the office of sheriff for less than a year. Sol felt no regret at relinquishing the position to the long-serving deputy. At the time, Clint had taken the mantle with eagerness.

"You might as well get some sleep. Nothing to be done before dawn," Sol said.

Clint stared at the maps as if they would tell him something new. "The parents aren't sleeping."

Above them, a long rumble of thunder rolled its way across the sky. Sol prayed without faith that the storm would take pity on the missing boy, named Benjamin, and pass them by. His fingers hovered over the topographical map, showing the elevation gains. Clint stood, but before he could walk away, Sol's finger jabbed the map. "He's here. Probably up one of three draws. I'll head out at dawn."

Clint wouldn't question Sol's assertion. He'd found other missing people without taking a step outside. "Do you want to take some of the crew with you?" His resigned tone held no expectation of a yes.

"No, I'll go alone. I don't want to chance anyone stomping over tracks." He looked up, and a rare smile crossed his face. "I'll have him back by lunch."

* * *

Jennifer stood next to one of the bonfires—in the group but not part of it. She recognized Chapa's van immediately from the last search she'd been a part of. As the headlights shined on her, she turned away and faced the flames.

Her body tensed as he jumped out, his long legs landing in a puddle, and she waited for him to approach the group. The parents of the missing boy sat huddled not far from her. He would want to speak with them, question them.

The slamming of the motorhome door proved her assumptions wrong.

Relief flooded her. She'd met Sol Chapa once at another search that hadn't ended well. In fact, it had almost ended in her arrest—an event she was not eager to repeat.

Coming here and chancing being recognized was foolhardy and risky. Two adjectives that described much of her previous ten years.

A man next to her shivering in shorts and a t-shirt offered a quiet smile. "I didn't catch your name. Which part of the family do you come from?"

Family of the missing outnumbered searchers, most of whom had gone home or retired to tents for the night. "Oh, we're the black sheep."

He chuckled before glancing around in shame and lowering his voice. "I thought that was us." His light tone meant he must be a more distant relative to the boy.

"Not even close. I should go check on my lambs." She retreated before he could ask anything else. She wanted information about the search but not attention.

A few drops of rain fell on her jacket, and she pulled the hood up over her head. Had coming here been a mistake? If so, she refused to admit it just yet.

She'd been a hundred miles away when she'd heard about the missing child. At first, she'd ignored her internal compass pointing her back to Lost Gorge—after all, what did this kid have to do with her? Despite her best intentions, a day later found her out on the highway thumbing a ride to the mountains she'd spent years running away from. The missing kid had nothing to do with her. But she'd once been a child, too, in those forests, desperate to go home.

That wasn't the real reason she'd come. She risked everything on the off chance the searchers would find something beyond the kid. Something that would help her in her own search—a slim chance to be sure.

She did learn one thing around the campfire that night. Everyone thought the caves were too far away and too high of a climb for an eight-year-old. She knew differently. And a boy on an adventure might stumble into something he shouldn't.

Let Chapa and everyone else search the forests—she would go underground.

About the Author

Lee is an analyst by day, writer by night, and ski instructor by weekend. All of that makes her sound way more awesome than she is, but that's the point. Most of her stories include some outdoor element since that's where her best ideas come from. Follow her adventures at weekendwomanwarrior.com.

You can connect with me on:
- https://weekendwomanwarrior.com
- https://twitter.com/WeekendWomanWar
- https://www.facebook.com/WeekendWomanWarrior
- https://www.instagram.com/weekendwomanwarrior
- https://www.pinterest.com/mkdymock

Subscribe to my newsletter:
- https://mailchi.mp/1a0cfaa61f57/weekend-woman-warrior

Made in United States
Orlando, FL
12 January 2023

28605374R00126